Dodd, Mead & Company
New York

Morning Star, Black Sun

MORNING STAR,

BLACK SUN

The Northern Cheyenne Indians
and America's Energy Crisis

Brent Ashabranner

Photographs by Paul Conklin

This book is for Miller Crazy Mule, Tom Gardner, Jr., Anthony Littlewhirlwind, Pamela Little Wolf, and all other young Northern Cheyenne, who hold the future of the tribe in their hands.

Picture Credits: Smithsonian Institution National Anthropological Archives, pages 14, 15, 28, 39, 44–45, and 103.

1   2   3   4   5   6   7   8   9   10

Library of Congress Cataloging in Publication Data

Ashabranner, Brent K., 1921–
    Morning star, black sun.

    Bibliography: p.
    Includes index.
    Summary: Discusses relations between the Northern Cheyenne Indians of Montana and the United States government, as well as the tribe's recent fight to save its lands from strip-mining coal companies.
    1. Cheyenne Indians—Government relations—Juvenile literature. 2. Cheyenne Indians—Mines and mining—Juvenile literature. 3. Indians of North America—Government relations—Juvenile literature. 4. Indians of North America—Montana—Mines and mining—Juvenile literature. 5. Coal mines and mining—Montana—Juvenile literature. [1. Cheyenne Indians—Government relations. 2. Indians of North America—Government relations. 3. Coal mines and mining—Montana. 4. Conservation of natural resources—Montana] I. Conklin, Paul, ill.
    II. Title.
    E99.C53A83   323.1'197   81-19501
    ISBN 0-396-08045-6   AACR2

Contents

Author's and Photographer's Note

In writing this book and taking the pictures for it, we had the help of many people. We would like to express our special thanks to Ted Risingsun who opened many doors for us and spent long hours with us on the Northern Cheyenne reservation in southeastern Montana. So many members of the tribe gave so generously of their time that we cannot name them all here, but we do wish to express our particular appreciation to Ralph Red Fox, Tom Gardner, Sr., Dennis Limberhand, Joe Little Coyote, Sylvester Knows Gun, Donlin McManus, and John Woodenlegs.

We would also like to acknowledge the valuable help of Earl Murray, land reclamation officer for the Western Energy Company, and Doug Richardson of the Council of Energy Resource Tribes.

We were able to tell the story of Sweet Medicine, the great culture hero of the Cheyenne, only briefly in this book. It is a story exceedingly rich in both oral and written tradition and has a number of variations. Among several written sources we consulted in our research, we found Peter J. Powell's monumental two-volume work, *Sweet Medicine,* particularly helpful.

—*Brent Ashabranner*
—*Paul Conklin*

A Long Fight Continues

TED RISINGSUN met us at the Billings airport and drove us to the Northern Cheyenne reservation, a two-hour journey over good and lightly traveled roads. A thin early spring snow fell, dusting the brown eastern Montana hills. The hills were not brown, actually, because the grass, the tawny color of a lion's hide, gave a golden cast to the snow. Now and then we could see small bunches of cattle grazing or huddling in sheltered draws; otherwise, the vast rolling plains seemed empty.

As we drove through the Crow Indian reservation which adjoins Northern Cheyenne land, Ted pointed to a river in the distance. "The Little Bighorn," he said. "Right there is where Custer and his troops were killed. The Indians were mostly Sioux, but there were some Cheyenne."

By the time we reached Lame Deer the sun was shining through big gaps in the clouds. Lame Deer is the administrative center for the Northern Cheyenne tribe, but it looks very much like other small rural communities in the American West today. The one main street was dusty even though the snow had barely stopped. At the crossroads where the highway intersects the main street, the town's only traffic light swayed in the wind. There was a sleepiness about the light's orange-blinking eye, and no one seemed to pay much attention to it. Occasionally, the peaceful atmosphere was punctured by the roar of a motorbike; each one seemed to carry two and sometimes three young Indian riders.

Some pleasant small houses, most of them painted vivid yellow, green, blue, and red, are clustered randomly around the town and on the surrounding hills. Ted told us that Lame Deer has no movie theater, but we could see television antennas on most of the housetops. There is an all-purpose store, a reminder of the general store or mercantile of early days. A gas station near the crossroads sells prepackaged sandwiches and soft drinks, but the place to eat, Ted said, was a little cafe on the road to the coal mining town of Colstrip.

As the tribe's administrative center, Lame Deer does have some special features. A two-story building on the main street houses the Northern Cheyenne tribal office. On the other side of the crossroads is the U. S. government Bureau of Indian Affairs building, where the Bureau's reservation superintendent and his staff are located. It is the biggest building in Lame Deer. The Dull Knife Memorial Community College, named for a great Northern Cheyenne chief, opened in Lame Deer recently.

A community health center and a senior citizens' center are the most attractive buildings in town. Ted pointed out to us that the senior citizens' center is designed in the shape of the Northern Cheyenne symbol for the morning star.

"The morning star was very important to our ancestors," Ted said. "It signaled the coming of the sun, and our people knew that the sun gave them life. Most Cheyenne think that Dull Knife was our greatest chief, and his real name was Morning Star. Dull Knife was just a name someone gave him, but it stuck."

At a little before noon we went to the tribal office to meet Allen Rowland, President of the Northern Cheyenne Tribal Council. Rowland was in a meeting with some members of the Council and the Council's legal adviser, but he broke off to say hello. Rowland listened as we explained why we wanted to tell the story of the Northern Cheyenne, but it was clear that his mind was on business.

"Stay here long enough to get the story straight," he said and went back to his meeting.

We have tried to get the story straight, in both words and pictures. It is the story, now more than a century old, of a small Indian tribe's bitter struggle to secure a piece of land that could be its own forever. It is the story, in this century and at this time, of the Cheyenne's fight to preserve their land and their culture, their special beliefs and way of life, while fitting themselves into the America of which they know they are a part.

The town of Lame Deer

The Northern Cheyenne's fight has brought the tribe into conflict with the United States government and with some of the largest and most powerful coal and energy corporations in America. The relentless determination of the Northern Cheyenne to challenge both the government and big business in pursuit of justice and their right to survive as a tribe has blazed a trail for all other American Indian tribes. Because of their example, Dr. Kenneth Ross Toole, a distinguished author and professor of Western American history at the University of Montana, has called the Northern Cheyenne the most important Indian tribe in America today.

The efforts of the Northern Cheyenne to preserve their culture are at their height today. But to understand what motivates this tribe of less than four thousand people, it is necessary to look back more than a hundred years to the proud history and tragedy of their ancestors, warriors and hunters of the Great Plains.

The story begins there.

The Cheyenne: Hunters of the Great Plains

L IKE the singing of the high prairie wind, word spread through Eagle Chief's camp. "Blue Thunder has killed a white buffalo. He has killed it with a single arrow. We must make ready for the sacrifice."

Soon Blue Thunder rode tall and proud into camp. The white buffalo hide was rolled and tied securely to his short, strong-muscled hunting horse. Blue Thunder rode straight to the center of the camp and dismounted. He stood silently waiting for the ceremony to begin.

Although no one in Eagle Chief's camp ever before had killed a white buffalo, and few until that moment even had seen the hide of a wondrous white creature, every Cheyenne in camp knew what must be done. If properly carried out, the sacrifice of the white buffalo hide to the sun would assure the success of all buffalo hunts throughout the long winter. But if the ceremony was wrong in any detail, great sorrow would come to the tribe.

Now Wolf Without Fear walked to the place where Blue Thunder stood. Even though Blue Thunder had killed the white buffalo, he could not touch the hide again until it had been taken from his horse by a warrior who had pulled an enemy from his horse in battle and killed him in hand-to-hand combat. Such a man was Wolf Without Fear, leader of the Red Shield Society. The warrior carried his fighting lance in his right hand, and he touched the buffalo hide with it before he took the hide from Blue Thunder's horse and spread it on the ground.

Then every man, woman, and child in camp came to look at the marvelous white buffalo hide, but no one touched it and no one spoke while they were in its presence. After that a large sweat lodge was built, and many old men of the tribe went in to cleanse themselves and pray.

Very early the next day, when the morning star signaled the rising sun, the most honored priest of the tribe began his prayers. As the sun rose, he took the white buffalo hide and tied it to a pole that had been put up for this ceremony. Then all the women in camp brought gifts of beads, moccasins, cloth, and many other things, and the priest tied each gift to the pole. As he did so, the priest asked the sun and Maheo, the All Father who lives in the sky, to accept the white buffalo hide and the gifts, to look with kindness upon the people of the tribe, and to send many buffalo to their hunting parties.

When the priest had finished, the sun stood bright

Cheyenne beadwork

and high overhead, and the people knew that Maheo and the sun were happy and that their prayers would be answered.

At that time, which was not much more than a hundred years ago, buffalo were the life blood of the Cheyenne and of many other Plains Indian tribes such as the Sioux and Comanche. The huge shaggy beasts that roamed the West provided almost all of the Indians' food, as well as hides for their clothes and for the lodges in which they lived. To the Cheyenne the buffalo were almost as important as the sun that shone, the rain that fell, and the clean prairie air they breathed.

It had not always been that way. Long ago the

Cheyenne lived in what is now the state of Minnesota, and their tribal name was Tsitsistas. They lived among the lakes and ate fish and trapped small animals. They raised corn and beans and squash like the Indians of eastern America. But under the pressure of larger Indian tribes from the east and north, they gradually moved west until they reached the Missouri River.

During the years of their migration the Tsitsistas were joined by a closely related group called the Suhtai, and in time they became one tribe. The name Cheyenne, which is what the tribe was called in later times, was given to them because for a number of years they lived along the Cheyenne River in South Dakota. But in their own language, their tribal name is still Tsitsistas.

The Cheyenne's first settlements on the Missouri probably were established in 1676, one hundred years before the American colonists, half a continent away, declared their independence from England. In those days the Cheyenne knew almost nothing about a race of white men. To their sorrow, they would learn much about these people in the next two centuries.

In time the Cheyenne moved beyond the Missouri River and into the vast flat country that cuts a huge swath through middle America from Canada to Mexico. These are the Great Plains, an immense land of few trees and little rain, where the short-stemmed grass cured on the ground and in winter provided food for the great herds of buffalo that descended each year from the north.

When they first came to the Great Plains, the Cheyenne tracked and killed buffalo on foot, a terribly hard and dangerous task. Then from Indians far to the south they learned about horses, which were originally brought to America by the Spanish conquistadores. The Cheyenne traded for horses with the southern Indians, and they captured others from the herds of wild horses that roamed the plains. Very quickly the Cheyenne became superb hunters on horseback, and they developed a fierce mounted cavalry.

Over a long period of time the Cheyenne tribe developed two branches, a northern group and a southern group. No trouble brought about this split but rather a desire on the part of some to live in the flat, warmer Southwest, while others preferred the high rolling country of the Northwest. They remained one tribe in most beliefs and customs and often exchanged visits. Those of the north settled in and around the Black Hills of South Dakota, and their vast hunting range included the country lying toward Powder River, the Yellowstone, and the North Platte in Montana and Wyoming. These were the people who are known today as the Northern Cheyenne.

Although the Cheyenne did not have books, a system of writing, or schools, they had a tribal organization, codes of conduct, and ways of teaching their people that could rival those of any other society anywhere. The tribe was divided into ten groups or clans. While the different divisions had much in common, each also had its own taboos, ceremonies, and special medicines. In the governing tribal council each group was represented by four chiefs, and in addition there were four principal chiefs, making a tribal council of forty-four chiefs. This council decided all of the most

Group of mounted Cheyenne

serious tribal matters such as whether to move to new
hunting grounds, whether to make war on another
tribe, or whether to seek the special friendship of a
certain tribe. The chiefs representing the ten different
groups always listened to the feelings and views of
the people in their group so that the people's wishes
were known to the council of chiefs.

Chiefs were chosen for their wisdom, good judg-
ment, and bravery, though they did not necessarily
have to be great warriors. They did have to be good-
hearted men who were concerned about their people.

A young Cheyenne boy

(Overleaf) Present-day Cheyenne children. (Inset) Story time in Lame Deer

The very first duty of a chief was to see that widows and children without parents were well taken care of. His second most important duty was to be a peace-maker and to help in settling disputes within the tribe.

Wars were fought and defense of the tribe carried out by six warrior societies: the Fox Soldiers, Elk Soldiers, Dog Soldiers, Red Shields, Crazy Dogs, and Bowstrings. In addition, the chiefs formed a special fighting society. Each of these warrior societies had its own rules, ceremonies, dances, and battle gear.

The Dog Soldiers, for example, were made up of especially brave men, many of whom carried a cowhide rope ornamented with hawk or eagle feathers and a small, red-painted wooden stake on one end. If he dismounted to fight in battle, a Dog Soldier might thrust this stake into the ground. When he did so, he could not retreat behind it, no matter how badly the fight might be going. He had to stand his ground and fight to the death unless some other member of the tribe pulled up the stake, permitting him to retreat with honor.

The warrior societies included most of the able-bodied men of the tribe but not all of them, for no one was forced to join any of the groups. Boys as young as thirteen could join. In addition to their fighting duties, the warrior societies were responsible for seeing that tribal members obeyed the orders of the chiefs. But since the chiefs listened to the people in making their decisions, orders seldom were disobeyed. The warrior societies also had day-to-day duties, such as regulating hunting parties and seeing that the camp moved promptly.

Lame Deer schoolboys playing

Cheyenne children were taught by their mothers and fathers and other relatives, and nothing was considered more important than that the children of the tribe be brought up properly. In their younger years both boys and girls had plenty of time for play, but their games frequently took the form of pretending to hunt buffalo, to make camp, or to surprise the enemy. Both boys and girls were taught to be excellent riders and good swimmers. Boys improved their skill with bow and arrow from an early age and joined real buffalo hunts by the time they were in their early teens. Training in battle was given by an older experienced warrior who looked after a young boy on his first war party or in his first fight. Girls were taught by their mothers to dress hides, gather firewood, make clothes, pots, baskets, and perform the many other duties necessary to successful camp life.

For the Cheyenne the world of the Great Plains was a rich and good world which they thought would last forever. But the old people of the tribe knew that in the Cheyenne religion there was a voice that told them it would not last forever.

Sweet Medicine

IN the Cheyenne religion there is one supreme god, the Wise One Above, the All Father, whose name is Maheo and who lives in the sky. It was Maheo who made everything: the earth, the sun, the stars, the moon. He created people and put them on the earth, and then he put there all kinds of animals, birds, and fish. Maheo told the Cheyenne that these creatures were placed on earth for the benefit of mankind but that they must be respected and never killed needlessly.

Maheo has four spirit servants or helpers, each of whom dwells in one of the cardinal directions: north, where the cold wind comes from; south, where the cold wind goes; east, where the sun comes up; west, where the sun goes to sleep. Maheo and the four sacred spirits are always addressed in Cheyenne prayers, their help is asked in all private and tribal petitions, and the pipe is always offered to them first in the Cheyenne smoking ceremony.

As a people whose very lives were intertwined with all aspects of nature, the Cheyenne ascribed great mystical powers to the sun, moon, wind, rain, thunder, lightning, and other natural elements. They treated buffalo with great reverence, and they believed in the magical powers of many animals such as deer, elk, wolves, and coyotes, as well as the two fierce birds of prey, the eagle and the hawk.

Because of its intelligence, the coyote was greatly respected and considered especially sacred. It was believed that certain Cheyenne men had the power to talk to coyotes and to understand what coyotes said to them. The warrior Dives Backward was such a man. Once a coyote told Dives Backward that enemy raiders would attack the Cheyenne camp at dawn. The Cheyenne were ready when the attack came and drove off the enemy. Another time a coyote told Dives Backward exactly where a band of Pawnee was camped, and the warrior led a successful war party against this old enemy of the Cheyenne.

The Cheyenne considered the bald eagle to be the fiercest fighter of all living things, human or animal. Arrows made with the feathers of the bald eagle were thought to have special strength and magic. Some Cheyenne believed that if a bald eagle was killed, it would be dead for only four days. On the fifth day it would come alive and reoccupy its nest. Since the bald eagle knew that it would be dead for only a short time, it was not afraid of being killed.

Although all Cheyenne admired bravery, the

greatest hero in the legends and traditions of the tribe was not a warrior but rather a teacher and prophet named Sweet Medicine. At first his name was Sweet Root Standing, and it was a beautiful name, for the juice of the sweet root is drunk by new mothers to increase their milk.

Even as an infant Sweet Root Standing seemed to understand everything people said, and as he grew older it was clear that he knew many things that even the wisest chiefs in the tribe did not know. But the young man had a dispute with an important chief and left the tribe to wander alone on the prairie for four years. When Sweet Root Standing left his people, all of the buffalo, deer, antelope, and all other game also disappeared.

The Cheyenne went through four years of famine, and the people were near starvation when Sweet Root Standing came back to the tribe. He saw that there was no food and he said, "I will sing for four nights and call back the buffalo."

He had the people move their lodges into a perfect circle, and he went to the middle of the circle and sang for four nights, calling the buffalo. Then, as the sun rose on the fifth day, the people felt the shaking of the earth and they heard the drumming of many hooves. The buffalo had returned, and there was no more famine in the land. At that time Sweet Root Standing's name was changed by the people to Sweet Medicine because of the wonderful things he could do.

One other time Sweet Medicine left his people and again he was gone for four years. This time he took with him his wife, and they went into the land known as the Black Hills. At last they came to a small mountain with steep slopes and a large flat rock on the side from which they approached. Just as they reached the rock, the whole side of the mountain opened, revealing a huge room inside. Sweet Medicine went into the room without fear and his wife followed, also without fear because she was with her husband.

In the room inside the mountain were the four sacred helpers of Maheo, the All Father. They said to Sweet Medicine, "We have been waiting for you." And Sweet Medicine replied, "I have come."

On the ground in front of him Sweet Medicine saw four arrows tipped with feathers of the gray hawk. Nearby lay four more arrows tipped with feathers of the bald eagle. The sacred helpers said to Sweet Medicine, "Which arrows do you want?"

Both groups were beautiful arrows, but Sweet Medicine's eyes lingered on those with the eagle feathers. Their points were made of stone, as in the most ancient times, and their shafts were painted red and black with colors that came from the earth. "The eagle feathers are the ones I want," said Sweet Medicine.

Then the sacred helpers of Maheo gave Sweet Medicine the skin of a coyote to wrap the arrows in, and they taught him how the magic of the arrows, which were called Mahuts, could help his people in time of war. Sweet Medicine and his wife stayed inside the mountain for four years, and the sacred spirits taught him many more things to help his people. Then he returned with his wife to their tribe, and he taught the men, women, and children all that he had learned.

A Cheyenne arrowhead

He taught them the everyday things of life such as how to cook meat to avoid sickness and how to make baskets and weave cloth. He taught them the great laws of not stealing from or killing a brother tribesman or doing anything to bring shame to the Cheyenne. He taught the people much more, and he gave them Mahuts, the Sacred Arrows, and taught them their magic.

In the Cheyenne religion there was but one other great magical treasure that compared in power with the Sacred Arrows. That was the Sacred Buffalo Hat called Is'siwun. Is'siwun was made from the skin of a buffalo cow's head, to which a pair of shaved-down, decorated buffalo horns was attached.

25

Cheyenne legend tells that in ancient times the Buffalo Hat was given to Standing on the Ground, a great hero of the Suhtai branch of the Cheyenne tribe, by Maheo and his sacred helpers. Just as the sacred helpers had taught Sweet Medicine about Mahuts so did they teach Standing on the Ground about the Sacred Buffalo Hat, and they taught him how to dance the Sun Dance.

Standing on the Ground returned to the tribe and told the people to make a great medicine lodge. Then he taught them about the powers of the Buffalo Hat and showed them how to dance the Sun Dance. When the people saw Standing on the Ground wearing the Buffalo Hat with its horns thrust upward, they changed his name to Erect Horns.

The power of Mahuts, the Sacred Arrows, and of Is'siwun, the Sacred Buffalo Hat, was great. They were always carried when the whole tribe went into battle against an enemy. If the proper ceremonies were carried out, the Cheyenne people were sure that these great gifts from Maheo would bring them victory.

Sweet Medicine and Erect Horns had made it very clear to the people exactly what must be done to invoke the protective power of Is'siwun and Mahuts. Two young warriors must be selected, one to carry the arrows, the other to wear the hat. First the arrow carrier chewed a piece of root that was always tied up in the Sacred Arrow bundle. He blew the root in the direction of the enemy, and it was supposed to make them blind. Then the arrow carrier chanted songs and led the men of the tribe in a special dance that was performed only on that occasion.

After the ritual dance, the keeper of the Sacred Arrow bundle tied it to the lance of the warrior who would carry it in the fight. At the same time the keeper of the Sacred Buffalo Hat placed the hat on the head of the warrior selected to wear it and secured it with a rawhide thong under his chin. The two bearers of the sacred medicine relics then mounted the swiftest horses of the tribe and led the warriors into battle.

When the enemy was sighted, the bearer of the Sacred Arrows and the Buffalo Hat wearer charged swiftly ahead, but just before reaching the enemy fighters they turned toward each other, crossed, and rode a complete circle around their foes. This act would bring forth the power of the Sacred Arrows and the Buffalo Hat and was supposed to frighten and confuse the enemy and increase their blindness.

The early Cheyenne believed completely in the power of these two magic treasures, and the greatest reverence was shown them. Two of the most respected men of the tribe were selected as their keepers, and the Sacred Arrows and the Sacred Buffalo Hat each had a special lodge for its safekeeping.

In 1830 the Sacred Arrows were captured by the Pawnees because the arrow bearer rode straight into the Pawnee warriors instead of circling as he was supposed to do. Two of the arrows were later regained, and two substitute Sacred Arrows were made and blessed in a long and solemn ceremony.

Much later—some Cheyenne say that the year was 1869—the Sacred Buffalo Hat was damaged. Broken Dish, then the keeper of the hat, died and there was a dispute over who would become the next keeper.

The lodge of Is'siwun, the Sacred Buffalo Hat

The wife of Broken Dish tore a horn from the Buffalo Hat and kept it with her. Though the horn was taken from her and restored to the hat, every Cheyenne remembered that Erect Horns had told the people that no member of the tribe must ever damage or show disrespect to Is'siwun.

The loss of the Sacred Arrows and the mutilation of the Buffalo Hat shocked the Cheyenne more than anything that had ever happened in their history. The whole tribe mourned for months, even years, and many Cheyenne believed that the tragedies which befell the tribe in later years were caused by what had happened to their precious religious treasures.

It was after the arrows were lost and the hat was torn that the old men of the tribe began to recall the final prophecy that Sweet Medicine made at the time of his death many, many years before. It is said that Sweet Medicine lived the time of four long lives among his people, but at last he called the entire tribe to him and told them that he soon would leave them forever.

"Now I will speak to you," he said, "and you must listen well.

"I have brought you many things, sent by the gods for your use. Live the way I have taught you and follow the laws. You must not forget them, for they have given you strength and the ability to support yourselves and your families.

"Long ago the All Father spoke to me that he had put upon the earth all kinds of people. Someday, toward the sunrise, by a big river, you will meet a people who have white skin. They will be people who do not get tired but who will keep pushing forward, going, going all the time.

"Buffalo and all animals were given to you by the All Father, but these white people will come in and begin to kill them. They will use a different thing for killing—a stick that makes a noise and sends a little round stone to kill. In only a little time the buffalo will be gone.

"These people I tell you of will look for rocks that shine, rocks that the All Father put in the earth in many places. These people will want the land which the All Father has given to you, and they will try to take it from you.

"The white people will try to change you from your way of living to theirs, and they will keep at what they try to do. They will tear up the earth and at last you will do it with them. When you do this, you will become crazy and will forget all that I have taught you. Then you will disappear."

In that ancient time the people of the tribe listened quietly to Sweet Medicine. They loved him and knew of his powers and wisdom. But they had seen the plains covered with endless herds of buffalo, and no one believed that all of them could ever be killed. This time, the people said, even the great and wise Sweet Medicine must be wrong.

"We Can Make the Ground Bloody"

BUT Sweet Medicine was not wrong. Beyond the great river called the Missouri, the Cheyenne met men with white skin, and they met others in the Yellowstone country and along the Platte River in Nebraska. At first there were not many of them, and it was easy to keep away from them. Sometimes the Cheyenne even let a white man come into camp and eat roasted buffalo hump and sometimes go with them on a buffalo hunt. In those days, which was before 1850, the strange white people, who often had long hair on their faces, did not seem like the same men that Sweet Medicine had warned his tribe about.

Then, with a terrible swiftness, everything changed. In twenty-five years between 1850 and 1875, the trickle of white-skinned people into the Great Plains became a stream and then a river. Most hated were the buffalo hunters who came with rifles and slaughtered the buffalo by the tens of thousands. They

took only the hides and left the carcasses to rot and the bones to whiten on the plains.

Many more white-skinned people came, not only men but also their wives and children. They built sod houses on the prairie and plowed the ground to plant corn, wheat, and vegetables. They brought animals that were like buffalo and yet not like them, and these creatures ate the grass that once only the buffalo had eaten. Men came to build railroads, and wherever their endless tracks stretched, farmers and ranchers came to live around them.

In so little time the buffalo were gone, and the places where the Cheyenne and the other Plains Indians had hunted deer, antelope, and other game were now places claimed by the white people. The government in Washington tried to set aside certain lands that would be only for the Indians, but always the white people kept coming, and the Indians fought for what had first belonged to them.

Then came the blue-clad soldiers, and the years of death and despair began for the Cheyenne and all other Western Indians. The soldiers were not great horsemen as the Indians were, but they rode well and had many mounts. They carried fine light guns called carbines, guns that could fire many times without reloading. These soldiers were many and they rode against the Indians from a string of forts that stretched down the Great Plains from Fort Keogh in Montana to Fort Sill in Oklahoma and on beyond to Texas.

Buffalo were important to the Cheyenne way of life

Some chiefs knew that the arrow and lance could never win against the carbine, and they tried to keep the young warriors from raiding farms and ranches of settlers and from attacking patrols of soldiers. Such a chief was Red Cloud, the great peace chief of the Sioux, and such were the Cheyenne chiefs, Black Kettle, Little Wolf, and Morning Star, who was always called by his other name, Dull Knife.

Black Kettle believed that he had a peace agreement with the U. S. Army, but at dawn on a bleak November morning in 1864, his camp on Sand Creek in eastern Colorado was attacked by cavalry and cannon. Of 123 persons killed in the surprise attack, 98 were women and children. Fighting a desperate rear guard action, Black Kettle and his warriors helped most of their people escape, but with no possessions and only the clothes they wore. Some of the soldiers in the raiding party were deeply disturbed by what they had seen and made their feelings known to Congress and the War Department in Washington. An investigation was held, but the commanding officer of the Sand Creek Massacre, as the attack has become known in history, was not punished.

Even after Sand Creek, Black Kettle did not cease to try to find a way for his people to live in peace with the whites. But four years later on the banks of the Washita River in Oklahoma, at dawn on a cold November morning, his camp was again attacked and his people killed without mercy, with women and children as much the targets as the warriors of the tribe.

This time Black Kettle died in the attack, and there were those who said that he stood in front of his lodge as if he no longer wanted to live. The attack on Black Kettle's camp on the Washita was made by the army's Seventh Cavalry, and its leader was a man the Indians called Long Hair. To the white world he was known as General George Armstrong Custer.

After the attack on Black Kettle, Dull Knife and Little Wolf led their people deep into the Dakota Black Hills. There they hoped that the whites would not follow and they might live as the Cheyenne had lived in times past. But that was not to be. In 1874 General Custer led an army reconnaissance mission into the Black Hills and reported evidence of gold in a number of places. Then the Cheyenne remembered the words of Sweet Medicine, for white men began to pour into the sacred hunting grounds of the Sioux and Cheyenne in search of the stones that glitter.

At that time word went out from the army that all Indians in the Black Hills must report to army agencies, where they would be assigned to live on reservations. If they did not come in, they would be considered hostile and would be hunted by the army.

There was no reservation in the north for the Cheyenne, and they were to be sent to the Cheyenne reservation in Oklahoma to live with the southern branch of their tribe. Even Dull Knife and Little Wolf, the peace chiefs, knew that their people could not live in that hot southern place where there were already too many people and no game to hunt. Like silent shadows the Cheyenne moved from the Black Hills into the rolling country of eastern Montana and hoped they could stay away from the soldiers.

On a creek called Rosebud that hope died. The

ALL WE ASK IS TO BE ALLOWED TO LIVE....
AND TO LIVE IN PEACE. DULL KNIFE

*A reminder of the great chief Dull Knife appears
in a school today in Lame Deer.*

War Department decided that the Indians must be
punished for not reporting to the army agencies as
they had been told to do. General George Crook and
General Alfred H. Terry moved out with strong forces
on this punishment mission. Terry moved southward
from the Yellowstone, while Crook worked northward
and covered the headwaters of the Powder, Tongue,
and Bighorn rivers and Rosebud Creek.

Crook found a large encampment of Cheyenne
near the Rosebud, but the sharp-eyed Cheyenne scouts
had found the soldiers first, and word went back to
the villages to be prepared. If this had not been June,
the moon of making fat, if the Cheyenne had not loved

this valley so much with its clear stream and hills of pine, juniper, and chokecherry, they might have struck their lodges and slipped away.

If Dull Knife or Little Wolf had been present, perhaps the decision would have been to vanish into the hills rather than fight. But these two chiefs were with their people on the Yellowstone, and the Cheyenne on the Rosebud were led by fiery men like Two Moons and Comes in Sight. With them were some of the bravest warriors of the tribe: White Shield, Little Hawk, Yellow Eagle, Crooked Nose, and White Bird. And so the ancient battle cry rang out, "The sun shines brightly, and it is a good day to die!"

The fight took place in the hills along the Rosebud and in a level meadow where the creek makes a large bend. Although there were not many casualties on either side, the battle was a hard one, and at last Crook, in fear of being led into a trap, gave the order for his troops to retreat. It was a victory for the Cheyenne.

During the battle Chief Comes in Sight charged the soldiers many times and rode up and down the line as if daring the enemy to hit him. At last a bullet knocked his horse down, and Comes in Sight was thrown to the ground. Crow Indian scouts fighting for the army started down from the hills to kill the chief; but before they reached him, the sister of Comes in Sight, a girl named Buffalo Calf Road, mounted a swift horse and dashed to her brother. He swung onto the horse behind her and they escaped unhurt. In Cheyenne history, the fight on the Rosebud has always been called Where the Girl Saved Her Brother.

For the Cheyenne, proud warriors of the plains,

a fight on even terms in which they made the hated
Blue Coats retreat was sweet indeed. But they knew
that Crook had more troops to bring against them,
and they knew that Terry was moving into the area.
So quickly they broke their camp on the Rosebud and
joined a large gathering of Sioux not far away on a
river called the Little Bighorn.

Word of the battle on the Rosebud reached Dull
Knife and Little Wolf, and only a few days later came
news that shocked the entire country. Long Hair, General Custer, and over 250 troops of his Seventh Cavalry
riding as a part of Terry's force had been wiped out
in a great battle on the Little Bighorn. Most of the
Indians were Sioux, fighting under the brilliant war
chief Crazy Horse, but some of the warriors had been
Cheyenne who had fought just the week before on
the Rosebud. They had been led by Chief Two Moons.

Then the people said, "Now our time has come
again. Now the Blue Coats will leave us alone, and
we will retake the land that is ours." But Little Wolf
and Dull Knife told their people that it would not
be that way. They knew how strong the army was,
and they knew that the soldiers now would come in
a fury to drive them to the reservations or to kill them.

And these chiefs of the Cheyenne were right. Little Wolf, who would have made a great general if he
had worn a blue army coat, moved his people through
the hills all that summer and fall of 1876 with great
skill. But in late November a large army detachment
under General R. S. Mackenzie surprised Dull Knife's
village on Powder River and destroyed it. Little Wolf
was there, and he and Dull Knife fought fiercely and

Dull Knife (seated) with Little Wolf.

with part of their people escaped into the hills. But all of their food, clothes, and other possessions were lost. Little Wolf was wounded six times in the battle, but he did not die.

Without food, without their warm buffalo robes, blankets, and lodges, the cruel winter in that high, cold country brought the Cheyenne close to starvation and death from freezing. General Mackenzie sent word to them, asking that they surrender to him at Fort Robinson in northern Nebraska. He promised them food and shelter and a reservation of their own in the hunting country that had always been theirs.

Even then it was not until April of 1877 that Dull Knife and Little Wolf finally led their people numbering almost one thousand to the fort and placed themselves under the protection of General Mackenzie. Only when escape was hopeless did they learn that there was no reservation for them in their country. They also learned that the government of the white men was determined to make them go south to live with the Cheyenne in Oklahoma.

The Northern Cheyenne protest was bitter, and they refused to go south even when food was withheld. Only when they were told that they could go on a trial basis, that they could return north if they were not happy in the south, did they agree to make the long trek to Oklahoma. And so the unhappy journey from their homeland began. Most of the people were on foot, tired, still hungry, still poorly clothed. The women of the tribe wailed as they looked one last time at the hills which had given them and their children life, and tears came to the eyes of the strongest men.

The march to the Darlington Agency in central Oklahoma took seventy days, and the sultry heat of a Southwest summer lay like a blanket on the land when the people of the north arrived. From the beginning their life there was a disaster. There were too many people. There was no game to hunt, and the rations supplied by the government were barely enough to prevent starvation. In the hot heavy air the people of the north became sick, and their sickness was made greater by the swarms of mosquitoes and the ticks. When winter came the wind howled across the flat prairie; there were no buffalo to hunt for making robes and clothes, and the government supply of these things was pitiful. In too many lodges that winter the death wail was heard.

Worst of all perhaps, there was nothing for the young men and the young women to do. These men who had swept the plains hunting buffalo, who had tracked deer and elk in the northern hills, these women who had made clothing and blankets, who had taught their daughters to cook and care for the camp, now sat in sullen idleness watching each day drag slowly into the next.

Dull Knife and Little Wolf knew that their people were dying, that they could not live in this southern place under these conditions. In vain they pleaded with the Indian agent and with the army commander to let them return north, as they had been promised they could if they were not happy here. But always they

were told that they must stay and that the soldiers
would stop them if they tried to leave.

At last, when a year of misery had run its course,
they knew that the people must try to return to their
northern home even if everyone died in the attempt.
Little Wolf asked once more for permission for the
people to leave Darlington Agency and again he was
refused. Then he stood up and said to the agent and
to the army officers, "I am going to leave this place.
I am going north with my people to our home. I do
not want to see blood spilled on this agency, and if
you must send the soldiers against me, I hope you
will first let me leave here. If I must fight you, we
can make the ground bloody in some far place."

The soldiers watched Little Wolf closely, but one
moonless night he and Dull Knife and their people
moved silently out of camp. They left fires burning
so that they would make bright dots in the night, and
they left their lodges standing so that the soldier guards
would see them in the first light of dawn.

Little Wolf, a great planner and organizer, led the
long homeward trek, and it is one of the great stories
of American history. He moved the people fast for
two days and then hid them in the hills north of the
Cimarron River so they could rest. A patrol of soldiers
found them, but Little Wolf's small band of fighters
stood off the Blue Coats while the people moved out,
again at night, and escaped.

They forded the Arkansas River above Fort
Dodge, fought soldiers twice more and escaped as they
worked their way through Kansas, traveling mostly
at night but sometimes by day. They crossed the Kan-

sas Pacific Railroad and made their way to the South Platte River in southern Nebraska.

At that place Dull Knife and Little Wolf parted. Dull Knife took his people and most of the elderly and sick of the tribe and turned westward. It was his plan to find the reservation of Red Cloud, the Sioux, near Fort Robinson and ask this old friend for help. What Dull Knife did not know was that Red Cloud and his people had been moved north to the Dakotas. Now there was no place for Dull Knife to turn, and even as he learned about Red Cloud, a terrible blizzard struck. Starving, freezing, almost without clothes, Dull Knife and his people were again forced to surrender at Fort Robinson, the place from which their tragic journey to Oklahoma had begun a year and a half ago.

At Fort Robinson the Cheyenne were told that they would again be sent south to Oklahoma. They were locked up and held without food and water to make them agree to go. But Dull Knife and his people knew that they would rather die than live in that place as virtual prisoners, and they made a final, desperate run from the fort for freedom. Most were killed by the soldiers or captured, but Dull Knife and a few tribesmen escaped, and they made their way, almost dead with cold and hunger, to the Pine Ridge Agency where Red Cloud and his fellow Sioux lived. There Dull Knife and his people were allowed to stay.

When Little Wolf left the South Platte River, he led his people through Nebraska with such skill that they were not found by the army. They crossed from Nebraska into South Dakota and hid in the Black Hills,

"The Escape of the Cheyenne Indians from the prison at Fort Robinson," from Frank Leslie's Illustrated Newspaper, *vol. 47, February 15, 1879.*

where Little Wolf knew the Blue Coats, in winter, could not find them.

In the spring of 1879 Little Wolf led his people to the Little Missouri River northwest of the Black Hills. It was there that an army officer he trusted, Lieutenant W. P. Clark, persuaded Little Wolf to bring his people to Fort Keogh on the Tongue River in Mon-

tana. The Cheyenne knew this country and loved it. It was a beautiful land with hills, pine trees, rolling grasslands, and water. At that time there were still some buffalo to be found there. So long as they did not try to leave the area, General Nelson A. Miles, the army commander, let Little Wolf and his people hunt and live in the hills around the Tongue.

And so Little Wolf's great work was done. He had brought his people, most of them on foot, a journey of fifteen hundred miles from the hated south back to their high northern home. On that journey he had eluded ten thousand army troops, except for three fights which he could not avoid and none of which he lost. He had forded rivers, crossed railroads, and worked his way around a string of forts and many towns. He had hidden his people in the sand hills of Nebraska and the Black Hills of Dakota so that no army scout could find them. It was a feat of which any great general could have been proud.

Finally, in 1884, mainly through the work of General Miles, the Northern Cheyenne were given their own reservation on the Tongue River. Then Dull Knife and his people were allowed to come from Pine Ridge, and the Cheyenne who had been kept at Fort Robinson after they were captured were allowed to come. The people were together again at last.

The reservation was small, 378,000 acres, where once the Cheyenne had roamed 350 million acres. But it was theirs, and never again did they yield their land to the white man. In fact, the reservation was enlarged so that today it is 460,000 acres, still small but still a piece of the earth that the Northern Cheyenne can call their own.

On the White Man's Road

A S the Cheyenne came onto their new reservation, they pitched their tepees in the hills and along the Tongue River or on Rosebud Creek and other creeks that flow through what was now their land. These people were poor almost beyond imagining. In the years of fighting and eluding the army, in the long marches to Oklahoma and back, they had lost almost all of their possessions, and there had been little opportunity to hunt buffalo, deer, and elk and to cure hides for making clothes and lodges.

There had been no chance to replenish their horse herds, and few had weapons, except for bows and arrows. Some did not even have lodges and had to build cabins, although they had but a few tools given them by the Indian Bureau and no experience at building white men's shelter.

Although their land was beautiful and the love of it ran deep in their blood, the early years of reserva-

tion life were a time of great hardship for the Cheyenne. The last of the buffalo were gone within the
first year or two, and there were not enough deer and
small game to feed the tribe. Furthermore, many of
the wild animals fled from the reservation under the
pressure of being hunted, and now the Indians could
not follow them.

Their ancestors in Minnesota had been farmers,
but as hunters of the plains the Cheyenne had "lost
the corn," as they said in their language. Now, in this
land of little rain where farming was a hard and doubt-
ful business, their first efforts to regain the skills of
tilling the soil were not successful. They existed on
wild berries and fruits, on what wild game they could
kill, but mainly on a ration of beef given out twice a
month by the Indian Bureau. It was a beginning of
dependence on the government—a dependence shared
by most American Indian tribes—that has lasted
throughout the twentieth century.

Slowly, however, life on the reservation began
to improve for the Cheyenne. They learned to make
gardens and they raised corn, pumpkins, potatoes,
peas, beans, and other vegetables. They learned to grow
hay in the river and creek bottoms and sold it by the
wagon load to agency headquarters and to ranches surrounding the reservation. Some of the young Cheyenne
men went to work for the ranches and learned about
cattle raising. Others made money cutting and selling
firewood, and some worked as freight haulers.

The Cheyenne had long known how to raise and
care for horses. Although most had been lost on the
long trek from Oklahoma, a few horses remained with

Donlin McManus. Horses have always been an important part of the Cheyenne way of life.

the tribe, and they were brought to the reservation. The reservation with its grasslands and sheltered hills was a fine place for raising horses, and in time many families had a hundred head and in some cases many more. The horses were of good quality, and many were sold to the government and to ranchers in eastern Montana. These sales provided another good source of income for the Cheyenne, but more than anything horses were a link to the past when the men of the tribe had ridden as proud warriors and hunters. In Cheyenne memory this period of reservation life is known as the Time of the Horse.

In a very wise move in 1903 the Indian Bureau brought a thousand cows and forty bulls to the reservation and divided them among all Cheyenne who were interested in raising cattle. Most of the Cheyenne men accepted this offer eagerly and quickly proved themselves to be excellent stockman. They were already skilled horse raisers, and some of the young men had learned about cattle. Cattle raising was in every way a good occupation for the Cheyenne.

Old people of the tribe always called the years from about 1903 to the early 1920s "the good years." The horse herds were in excellent condition. The original one thousand cattle increased to twelve thousand by 1912 and brought good prices on the market. Cheyenne women learned to can fruit and vegetables, ensuring a better winter diet; and solid log cabins, good family homes, began to dot the hills and valleys of the reservation. People were still poor and there were not many jobs for the young men, but a hopeful beginning had been made.

The Cheyenne were learning the white men's ways, but they did not forget their old ways. Elders of the tribe still smoked the medicine pipe and offered prayers to Maheo. The Sacred Buffalo Hat was carefully stored in its special tepee under the watchful eye of a keeper. The Sun Dance was still held, and other dances as well, such as the Buffalo Dance and

Buffalo Skull in front of Deer Rocks

the Shield Dance. People went to the Sacred Deer Rocks near the reservation to pray and make offerings for good health. Others travelled 150 miles to the east in South Dakota to visit the sacred Cheyenne mountain of Bear Butte and to receive instruction in the religion and traditions of the tribe.

And there were times to enjoy. Horse races were held regularly at Lame Deer and another reservation town called Busby. Powwows and social dances were held several times a year. One of the nicest old Cheyenne traditions carried on during this time was the giveaway. Families or communities that were doing well would announce a giveaway, and neighbors, friends from any place, and even people from other tribes were welcome to come. The family or community having the giveaway would provide abundant food for all who came. Then gifts of food, clothing, and even horses would be given to guests, to the accompaniment of singing and dancing. Sometimes giveaways were put on in memory of a family member who had died, but mostly they were a way to share one's good fortune with others.

John Woodenlegs is an elder of the Cheyenne tribe. He lives today near Lame Deer, raises cattle and teaches a course in Cheyenne history at Dull Knife Memorial Community College. Mr. Woodenlegs' grandfather was a great hunter and so strong that he once carried a freshly killed elk on his shoulders. His hunting companions were amazed at his strength and said that he surely must have legs as strong as trees. That was the origin of the family name Woodenlegs.

When we met Mr. Woodenlegs he talked at first

A modern-day powwow in Birney

about the early part of the century. "They may have
been the good years, but they weren't always so good
for the children," he told us. "The Indian Bureau
started schools, and the Cheyenne children were sent
away to them. The teachers wanted to make us into
white children. They wouldn't let us talk about our
homes or play Indian games or wear Indian clothes.

John Woodenlegs

We were taught that everything Indian was bad. If we said even one word of Cheyenne or any other Indian language, we were slapped or our ears were pulled. We didn't know any English, but that was the only language used in the schools. If we didn't do everything we were told to do, we were punished. Well, I learned English, but I always thought there should have been a better way to run those schools."

In 1914 the Indian Bureau made a decision that was later to result in disaster for the Cheyenne. The decision was that the herds of cattle owned by individual Cheyenne should all be combined in one large tribal herd. Individuals would continue to own their cattle and have their own brands, but the tribal herd would be under Bureau management. The Indian Bureau officials believed that with one large tribal herd the use of reservation grass could be better planned and round-ups and marketing more efficiently carried out. The Cheyenne protested bitterly. They did not want to give up the right to supervise and care for their own cattle. But the Bureau's decision was law, and the Cheyenne had to give up their cattle or have them taken away by force.

In 1919 another heavy blow fell on the Cheyenne, and it marked the beginning of the end of the good times. Again it was an Indian Bureau decision, and this one struck at the very heart of the Cheyenne way of life. The Bureau decided that the Cheyenne must reduce sharply the number of their horses in order to make more grass available for the tribal cattle herd. Perhaps it was necessary for some decision to be made about how many cattle and how many horses the Cheyenne would have, but the Cheyenne themselves had no voice in the matter.

Instead, the Bureau ordered one hundred Cheyenne horses a month to be shot and used for the monthly meat ration. At the same time some of the best horses on the reservation were rounded up and shipped to buyers in other parts of the country. In many cases the Cheyenne owners were paid nothing

for these horses that were shipped away. The Cheyenne were very angry. The love of horses ran almost
as deep in their blood as their love of the land, and
it was in horses that they had always counted their
personal wealth. Many of the young men of the tribe
tried to hide their horses, and some risked going to
jail to keep them. In time, however, all Cheyenne families lost most of their horses. In a matter of a few
years the number of Cheyenne horses dropped from
fifteen thousand to three thousand.

If possible, the tragedy of the Cheyenne cattle
was even worse. The Indian Bureau's agency superintendent had promised the Cheyenne when they turned
their cattle into the tribal herd that there would be
twenty thousand head within five years. Instead, the
size of the herd began to decrease almost immediately.
Without the attention of the individual owners, it was
too easy for cattle to disappear, to be killed by wolves,
and to starve or freeze in the hard Montana winters.

The final tragic chapter was written when the Bureau built a fence on the north-south ridge across the
reservation. The tribal herd was to be grazed on the
west side of the fence during the spring and summer
and on the east side during the fall and winter. In
the especially bitter winters of 1919 and 1920 the
Cheyenne owners wanted to get their herds back so
they could feed them hay and look after them, but
the Bureau refused their pleas. A number of Cheyenne
were sent to jail when they tried to get their cattle.
In those cruel winters cattle piled up against the fence
and died by the thousands.

John Woodenlegs has told the story many times,

and he told it once more to us. "That fence was pure ruin for the Cheyenne in the cattle business," he said.

He paused and a sad and distant look came into his eyes as if he could see the long, snow-covered death ridge. "The cattle wore a path along that fence. It was so deep you could see it for years. They knew where home was, but they couldn't get there."

"You Don't Sell Your Homeland"

I N 1924, without ever admitting the failure of its tribal herd policy, the Indian Bureau discontinued the program and gave the surviving cattle back to their owners. Out of about twelve thousand cattle originally given over to the Bureau by the Cheyenne, probably fewer than three thousand were returned. Some owners who had turned over hundreds of cattle to the tribal herd had twenty-five or thirty head returned to them. Many owners did not get back a single cow.

So few Cheyenne cattle were left that the Bureau leased the grazing rights to over a third of the reservation's best grassland to ranchers in the area. The lease price was only 10 cents an acre, yet even that money did not go to the Cheyenne. The Indian Bureau had run up debts in its handling of the tribal herd, and the lease money was used to pay those debts.

Some Cheyenne continued to raise cattle, but their financial setbacks were severe, and their spirit and drive were weakened. Then came the great American depression of the 1930s, and almost all markets for cattle and horses disappeared. The good times were over.

Even before the depression, the Indian Bureau had presented the Cheyenne tribe another problem to struggle with. An old law passed by the U. S. Congress in 1887 had given all American Indian tribes with reservations the right to divide their land among tribal members, with each member to receive 160 acres. That acreage would belong to the individual, and after a twenty-five year waiting period the person could sell it if he wanted to. Any land left over after the division of land to individuals would be owned by the tribe as a whole, just as it had from the beginning of the reservation system.

Whether or not to divide the reservation was left to each tribe to decide. Many tribes in America divided their land, and many Indians sold their share. Reservations became checkerboards of pieces of land owned by outsiders and those still owned by tribal members. There were cases in which all members of a tribe sold their land, and the reservation completely disappeared.

The Northern Cheyenne had never divided their land. Feeling ran deep among them that this land that they and their fathers and grandfathers had fought and died for belonged to the Cheyenne people as a whole and that it should not be cut up into little pieces for individual ownership. That was not the Cheyenne way of thinking about the land.

But in the late 1920s officials of the Indian Bureau began to try to persuade the Northern Cheyenne that

A cattle ranch in winter

they should divide their reservation land among the tribal members. They argued that a system of private ownership was better, for then the harder working and more ambitious persons could get ahead on their own. The Bureau seemed to have forgotten that it had acted just opposite of that principle in taking away individual cattle herds and starting a tribal herd. The Bureau also did not seem to realize that there was not enough good river and creek bottom land for everyone and that no family could make a living on 160 acres of dry grazing land.

For several years the Northern Cheyenne resisted the urging of Indian Bureau staff to divide their reservation; but then they were told that if they did so, the individual owners could receive government loans to improve their property. That was a powerful temptation and seemed to offer a promise of development, and in 1933 the tribe decided to give each of the 1,457 members of the tribe a tract of 160 acres. That left a little less than half of the reservation still owned by the tribe as a whole.

In 1932 the Indian Bureau changed its name to the Bureau of Indian Affairs and ever since has been known to all American Indians as the BIA. By law the BIA is the *trustee* of reservation lands owned by all Indian tribes in America. Indian land is *entrusted* to the Bureau, an agency of the United States government, to see that it is used in the best interests of the Indians to whom it belongs. Land is their most precious possession. Unfortunately, the record of the Bureau from the very beginning of its trusteeship has shown that too often it has not understood Indians and has not acted wisely in their behalf.

Like millions of other Americans during the depression years of the thirties, many Northern Cheyenne worked on government projects such as road building, dam construction, and improvement of national parks and forests. Because of government work programs like the Work Projects Administration and the Civilian Conservation Corps probably more Northern Cheyenne than ever before had jobs and a steady cash income, but these were very low-paying jobs and did not provide any extra money to improve their property. In fact, many families left their land and moved to the towns of Lame Deer and Busby during this period.

In 1941 America entered World War II, and eighty-two young Northern Cheyenne men and four women joined the armed forces, just as many of their fathers had during World War I. Others left the reservation to work in war plants or take other jobs made abundant by the war. Still others fought in the Korean War of the early fifties.

Most of the tribal members who left the reservation returned, but some did not. In general, the period beginning with the depression in 1930 through the 1950s was a prolonged time when there was little or no development on the reservation. It was a time of listless inactivity, and Lame Deer became a town of shacks, deep-rutted unpaved streets, and the rusting hulks of worthless cars. It was also a time, especially during the fifties, when the BIA began to encourage more Indians, including the Northern Cheyenne, to leave their reservations.

One of the Indians who listened to the Bureau was Ted Risingsun. Ted was born on the Northern Cheyenne reservation and first left it to serve in World War II. He left again to fight in the Korean War, and there he saw combat duty. When he came back to the reservation from Korea, his family had a victory dance for him with drumming and singing, as has always been done for Cheyenne men when they return from battle.

Ted was glad to be home. "I used to dream about these hills when I was in Korea," he told us during one of our long drives across the reservation. "When I was a boy, my father worked all over the reservation. Sometimes he cut trees for the sawmill. Sometimes he herded cattle. He took any job he could get. My mother and I went with him every place. We lived in a tent so we could be together all the time.

"But after I'd been back for a while, I guess I started looking at it with different eyes. There wasn't a paved road on the reservation, and that was in 1952. Lame Deer and Busby sure didn't look like the places I'd seen when I was in the army. Just about everyone on the reservation was poor and finding any kind of job was hard.

"People from the BIA talked to us, mostly the younger ones like me, about leaving the reservation and going out where the jobs were. They said Indians ought to get into what they called the mainstream of American life and not hide away by themselves on a

Car repair class at Dull Knife Memorial College

reservation. Well, I listened and I decided to go to St. Louis. I don't know why I picked St. Louis except that I knew some Cheyenne who had gone to places like Chicago and San Francisco, and I guess I wanted to do something different.

"The BIA made it real easy for an Indian to leave the reservation. The government had what they called relocation centers in some of the big cities. When we had picked a place we wanted to go, the BIA gave us travel expenses and money to live on for the first month while we looked for a job. The relocation center was supposed to help us get settled and find work.

"I found a two-room place I figured I could afford in the basement of a big apartment building in St. Louis. But when a man from the relocation center came to look at it, he said it wasn't good enough and that it might give a bad image to the relocation program. He made me give up that place and said he would help me get in a better one. But he couldn't find a landlord who would accept me in a bigger, more expensive apartment because I didn't have a job yet. So I tried to get my two-room place back, but it had been rented to someone else. That was all the help I got from the relocation center."

Ted Risingsun did find a job, and he learned that he could work and live away from the reservation. But he learned something else: He didn't want to live away from it. He returned and today lives with his family in Busby. He works for the Mennonite Indian Leaders' Council. He has a daughter attending Dull Knife College, and he has a grandson. What he wants more than anything is to see that this little Northern Cheyenne piece of the world is a good place for them to live.

In a general way, Ted Risingsun's story is similar to that of many others who have left the reservation only to return to stay. The pull of the land is powerful and runs deep in Cheyenne blood. Even those who have made their lives in other parts of the country almost always come back to visit and sometimes to take part in the sacred ceremonies.

Only a tiny part of Northern Cheyenne land ever

Welding student at Dull Knife Memorial College in Lame Deer

has found its way into the hands of outsiders. In the late 1950s, after the twenty-five year restricted period had passed, there was great pressure on the individual Cheyenne owners to sell their land. Some BIA officials even encouraged the Indians to sell. Yet today less than 2 percent of the reservation is owned by nontribal persons, and eventually all of it probably will be back

Bear Butte

in Northern Cheyenne hands because of a vigorous
tribal land acquisition program.

When a Cheyenne feels he has to sell his land,
he offers it first to the tribe. Although always desperate
for money, the tribal government has in every case
found a way to make the purchase. Today about 70
percent of the reservation is again owned by the tribe

69

Tongue River Valley

in common. The Northern Cheyenne reservation is one of the very few in the country that is still almost completely Indian owned.

Joe Little Coyote left the Northern Cheyenne reservation to get an education at Harvard University. It would have been easy for him to get a good job anywhere he wanted to live, but he returned to the reservation and took up important natural resource management work for the tribe. When we asked him why he came back, he didn't talk at first about the poverty of his people and how much needs to be done on the reservation. Instead he told us about something that happened almost a century ago.

"When General Miles—the Indians called him Bear Coat—decided to help my ancestors get a reservation," Joe Little Coyote said, "he picked a group of Cheyenne under Chief Two Moons and a troop of soldiers and told them to ride through the country until they found good land for a reservation. The Cheyenne rode straight to the Tongue River, and they said that was the land they wanted. The soldiers wanted them to look further, to be sure they had found the best place. They were afraid General Miles might think they hadn't done their job right. But the Cheyenne said, 'No. This will be our land.' "

Then Joe Little Coyote said, "Our spiritual history is here, in this land, and in Bear Butte where Sweet Medicine received the Sacred Arrows. This is more than a reservation. This is our homeland." And he added, "You don't sell your homeland."

After a moment of silence, Joe continued, "My grandfather and his father settled the Tongue River

Valley. When they first came there, they made a ceremonial fire place on which to build their lives and on which generations to come could build their lives. I still live on their land with my wife and five children. I carry on the sacred way the best I can and try to pass it on to my children."

The Tongue River forms the eastern boundary of the Northern Cheyenne reservation. It winds its way through a lovely valley of cottonwood, ash, and box elder trees, of meadows of hay and wheat. Plump-bodied pheasants try to hide in the brush along the riverbanks, but their bright green and red heads betray them to the watchful eye. At the time of full moon a soft white light washes river, brush, and trees; and in the first flush of dawn the morning star wavers in the sky like pale ghost fire.

If you have seen these things, if you have seen a deer work its way carefully down from the red and tan sandstone hills to eat the skunk sumac for which it has such a keen appetite, then you can understand more clearly what Joe Little Coyote is talking about. Then you think it is easier to know why he returned to the reservation which is really his homeland. You think you know why the Northern Cheyenne have never sold their land.

Coal: Black Shadow on the Land

A land beautiful but poor. From the beginning that short phrase has most accurately described the reservation of the Northern Cheyenne Indians. The stark sandstone hills topped with ponderosa pines are lovely, but they were not meant for the farmer's plow. The creek and river bottoms hold more promise, but they are limited and there is still not enough water. The one effort at irrigation was a disaster.

This is range country and the native grasses with names like blue gramma, thick spike, and prairie sand reed hold their own with sagebrush, yucca, and Indian paintbrush. These grasses are a wonderful graze for cattle; but it takes about thirty acres to nourish a cow and her calf for a year, and only a handful of reservation cattle raisers can make a decent living. The Northern Cheyenne Stock Growers Association carefully allots grazing rights, and there is always a waiting list.

No one has ever found gold, silver, or uranium in the reservation hills, and no pools of oil or fields of natural gas have yet been discovered. But geologists have known for a long time that the entire reservation is sitting on top of one of the richest fields of fossil fuel in the world. It is part of a gigantic block of virgin coal, called the Fort Union Formation, which extends from Canada through eastern Montana and Wyoming as well as North Dakota and part of South Dakota. The total reserves of the Fort Union Formation have been estimated at 1.5 trillion tons or about 40 percent of all the known coal reserves in the United States and 20 percent of all known world reserves.

Most coal reserves, however, cannot be mined with present-day methods and technology. What becomes important, therefore, is coal that can be mined easily. Coal on the Northern Cheyenne reservation has been estimated at between five billion and eight billion tons, a huge amount, and almost all of it can be recovered through strip mining. That means that the coal lies in vast sheets from about fifty to two hundred feet below the surface and can be reached simply by removing the soil over it. Expensive shafts and tunnels do not have to be dug.

But throughout most of this century the big coal companies of America had no interest in Northern Cheyenne or other Western coal because it was too expensive to move to the big coal-using industrial centers of the East and Midwest. Coal from West Virginia, Kentucky, Illinois, and Pennsylvania was cheaper. And so was oil, even oil imported from the Middle East or South America.

Strip mining at Colstrip

Some coal had been mined near the Northern Cheyenne reservation beginning in 1924. It was in that year that the Northern Pacific Railroad built the little town of Colstrip and began strip mining land owned by the railroad in order to supply coal for its steam locomotives. It was never much of an operation, just a little over a million tons of coal a year on the average, and the mining ended completely in 1958 when the Northern Pacific switched from steam to diesel-powered engines. In 1959 the Montana Power Company bought the coal leases, the machinery, and even the

Colstrip townsite from the Northern Pacific, but the power company did not resume mining.

Colstrip became a virtual ghost town, and only the "spoils," evil-looking little mountains of scooped-out earth, and the scars on the land where the coal had been removed gave evidence that mining had ever gone on there. It seemed that the final chapter had been written in a small and unimportant effort to mine coal in Western cattle country.

But it was not the final chapter. It was only the ending of chapter one. In 1966 the Northern Cheyenne Tribal Council received word that some coal companies might be interested in mining coal on their reservation. None of the Council members knew anything about coal mining, but the possibility of getting some money from coal was exciting. The Bureau of Indian Affairs urged the Tribal Council to lease as much land for coal mining as they could.

The Bureau developed a set of terms for coal exploration permits and mining leases, and public bidding was held in July, 1966. Only one company made a bid, but it was a giant of the American coal industry, the Peabody Coal Company. As a result of its bid Peabody received a permit to explore 94,000 acres of Northern Cheyenne land. After the exploration, the company could lease for coal mining any portion of the 94,000 acres it wanted.

The terms of leasing were set at the time the exploration permit was agreed to, and they seemed fairly simple. Peabody would pay the Northern Cheyenne tribe a royalty of 17½ cents for every ton of coal shipped off the reservation and 15 cents for every ton consumed on the reservation. There was also to be a bonus of 12 cents per acre covering the whole 94,000 acres of the exploration permit. That was not much money, just over $11,000, but Peabody officials pointed out that it was, after all, a bonus.

The Northern Cheyenne Tribal Council was puzzled as to why there should be a bigger royalty for coal shipped off the reservation than for coal used on the reservation. But the little bit of coal that the Cheyenne people might use did not seem to make any difference. It seemed to the Council that almost 100 percent of the coal would be shipped off the reservation. The Bureau of Indian Affairs expressed its satisfaction with the Peabody agreement, and the tribe approved it.

Peabody paid the small bonus and sent geologists to look over the land on which it now held an exploration permit. But Peabody officials were vague about when mining might get underway. There was some coal mining activity in the area, however. In 1969 the Montana Power Company reopened its Rosebud Mine near Colstrip, and after a ten-year sleep the little town came slowly back to life. Coal production was not much that year, just 150,000 tons, but there was talk that Montana Power had bigger plans in mind for Colstrip.

In the summer of 1969 the Bureau of Indian Affairs authorized another public bidding for Northern Cheyenne land for coal exploration permits and mining leases. Again the Peabody Coal Company was the only bidder, asking this time for a permit to explore 55,000 more acres. The terms of the permit and any future lease were the same as before. The Tribal Council wasn't sure why the big coal company wanted more land when it hadn't started to do anything with what it already had, but, with the Bureau's approval, the new exploration permit was signed. Peabody again paid the 12 cents an acre bonus but still seemed in no hurry to begin mining coal.

The year 1971 was one of startling developments in the story of Western coal. The Northern Cheyenne held a third public bidding for coal exploration permits and leases, and, with the Bureau of Indian Affairs encouragement, practically the whole reservation, except for the permits already held by Peabody, was divided into huge tracts and made available to bidders.

The result was a surprise and shock to the Tribal Council. This time there was not one bidder but twelve, big coal and power companies as well as individuals. As a result, large exploration permits were awarded to AMAX Coal Company and Consolidation Coal Company. Permits were also awarded to individuals who later sold them to Chevron Oil Company and Northern States Power Company. The acreage bonuses were larger in this third round of bidding, averaging about $9 an acre, but the royalty terms of 17½ cents and 15 cents a ton for coal remained the same. There was no change even though the U. S. Geological Survey had told the Bureau of Indian Affairs that the Northern Cheyenne royalty rates should be higher.

And so the situation in 1971 was this: five of the biggest energy companies in America, including Peabody Coal, had leases or leasing rights to over half of the entire Northern Cheyenne reservation.

Nor did the land hunger of the energy companies

stop with the Indians. Quietly they began to sign coal
mining agreements with ranchers in eastern Montana.
Some ranchers readily agreed to the leases, happy to
get big bonus money upon signing and to look forward
to years of coal royalties. Other ranchers resisted bitterly. This was their land, and their families had lived
on it from the time of the Indian wars. It was their
home. It was cattle country, and coal mining would
change it forever.

For now at least some idea of what the coal and
power companies had in mind was beginning to be
known. The Montana Power Company agreed to supply coal to utility companies in Minnesota and Wiscon-
sin and increased its coal production at the Rosebud
mine to over five million tons in 1971. Every day trains
of over a hundred cars were loaded at the mine and
hauled their black treasure eastward.

Even more significant—and to many people in
eastern Montana more alarming—Montana Power,
that same year of 1971, formed a partnership with
Puget Sound Power and Light Company of Washington State and began building two huge generating
plants at Colstrip. These plants, to be known as Colstrip One and Colstrip Two, would burn 2½ million
tons of coal a year from mines around Colstrip, and
each would be capable of generating 350 megawatts
of electricity. A megawatt is one million watts.

That meant that when the two mammoth plants
began operating in 1975 and 1976 their combined out-
put would be 700 million watts or enough electrical
power to fully meet the needs of ten cities of one
hundred thousand people each. Eighty percent of this

enormous amount of power would be used on the West Coast and would be sent there through transmission lines which would stretch in a straight line from Colstrip to Seattle.

But by far the most important coal development of 1971 was the publication by the U. S. Department of the Interior of a document called the *North Central Power Study*. The study was highly technical and hard to read, and, like most such studies, few people paid much attention to it. But those who did saw that plans were beginning that would completely change the way of life on the northern Great Plains.

The *North Central Power Study* was the joint work of the government and a number of large public utility companies in different parts of the country. What the study proposed was the stripping of billions and billions of tons of coal from the reserves in Montana, North Dakota, Wyoming, and elsewhere on the northern Great Plains and turning it into electricity by burning it in "mine mouth" generating plants, that is, plants built right beside the mines. The electrical power would then be sent around the country through a network of transmission lines.

The plan was a projection on a vastly larger scale of what was going to happen at Colstrip One and Two. The study proposed the building of forty-two generating plants, half of them in eastern Montana. These plants would be almost unbelievably big. The twenty-one in Montana would be capable of generating 69,000 megawatts. On the average every one of these plants would be almost ten times larger than Colstrip One and Two.

Colstrip power plants—with three towers standing

What had happened? Northern Great Plains coal had lain under the ground virtually untouched ever since Americans had had need for fossil fuels. As late as 1966, Bureau of Indian Affairs officials had called the Northern Cheyenne coal a "white elephant," implying that it had little or no value. Now private industry and the government were making plans to strip mine this coal on a scale that boggled the mind, a scale that far exceeded any coal mining operation the world had ever known.

Two things had happened. In the 1960s, years before most Americans had any idea of what was to come, energy experts knew that America could no longer meet its petroleum needs with domestic production. That inability, coupled with the political and economic changes taking place in the Middle East, was going to cause the price of oil to skyrocket. When that happened, the cost of turning coal into electrical power could compete with the cost of oil for the same purpose.

A greater concern for the environment was the second cause of the sudden interest in Great Plains coal. During the 1960s many new laws were passed to protect people, particularly in large cities, from the harmful wastes that result from industrial production and that come from the fumes of millions of cars, trucks, and buses. A new government department, the Environmental Protection Agency, was created to monitor the laws affecting air purity, river pollution, and other matters concerning a cleaner environment in which to live.

Coal is a dirty fuel. A big plant that burns coal

will every day spew into the air many tons of waste matter made up of tiny particles called particulate. Every day the smoke pouring from the giant stacks will carry tons of sulfur, sometimes hundreds of tons, and a huge amount of a dangerous gas called nitrous oxide.

Great Plains coal is much lower in sulfur content than most coal mined in the eastern part of the United States, and that made it more desirable in terms of the new clean air laws. But the dramatic idea that was now taking form was this: why not create electrical power in the sparsely populated Great Plains and ship it to the cities over transmission lines rather than ship coal to the cities and make the electricity in crowded urban areas? Even if modern technology could reduce harmful pollution in city plants, such a plan might be safer and cheaper.

Other questions still remained, of course. How would the people who lived on the northern Great Plains, the Indians, the ranchers, the townspeople, feel about having tens of thousands of acres of their land stripped bare and the coal blasted out? How would they feel about living beside a system of monstrous generating plants and a spiderweb of transmission lines? How would they feel about thousands of workers coming into the peaceful little cattle towns and changing them into coal mining and power plant towns? Not much thought was given to these questions by the energy experts. The first step was to get control of the coal by signing mining agreements with the people who owned the land. After that the power companies could consider the other problems.

One of the most puzzling questions was why the

Transmission lines—a symbol of Western power

Northern Cheyenne Indians signed over rights to more than half of their sacred land to the mining and power companies. This was land given to the Cheyenne by Maheo, the All Father. It was the land of Sweet Medicine, Dull Knife, and Little Wolf. These same Cheyenne who had signed the mining agreements had refused all temptations to move from the land or sell it to outsiders.

"We just didn't know what we were doing," one of the Tribal Council members told us. "We wanted money for the tribe. We didn't know what the coal companies were planning to do, and they sure didn't tell us."

Another former Tribal Council member said, "We didn't know anything about coal mining, and we didn't really think there would be much mining done. We did want those bonuses, though, and we didn't even realize how much of the reservation we were signing away. Mostly, though, those BIA people told us we were doing the right thing, and we trusted them. I don't think they gave us very good advice."

Much harsher words were leveled at the Bureau of Indian Affairs by Leah Margulies, a staff member of the National Council of Churches, who made a detailed study of the agreements between the Northern Cheyenne and the coal companies. Margulies wrote: "The BIA had led the Indians to the coal companies without giving them either the protection or information they badly needed." Margulies called the actions of the Bureau a betrayal.

Allen Rowland became president of the Northern Cheyenne Tribal Council in 1969 and still holds that position in the tribe. He is a big, serious man who sometimes limps when an old wartime shrapnel wound acts up. One of his early kin married a Cheyenne woman and was an early trader on the Tongue River before reservation days. Rowland was interested in the coal leases because they looked like some money for the tribe, and he knew as much as anyone about how poor his people were.

But slowly as that fateful year of 1971 drew to a close, Rowland and other elders of the tribe began to suspect that something was terribly wrong. It was not yet clear to them what was wrong, but that instinctive sense of tribal welfare that had guided the great chiefs of the past now began to trouble the thoughts and haunt the dreams of men like Rowland, John Woodenlegs, William Tall Bull, and Abraham Spotted Elk.

The tribe was in danger. They felt it in their bones.

"They Will Tear Up the Earth"

T HE Tribal Council chambers at Lame Deer were overcrowded and hot on that July day in 1972. Cheyenne from all over the reservation sat silently in their chairs and waited to hear the representatives of Consolidation Coal Company, known as Consol, explain the company's new offer. Most people in the room already had heard rumors of it, but the figures were so big that they were hard to understand.

The Consol team was large, and finally the leader stood up. He smiled and began to talk, first reminding the listeners that his company already had bid on and received a coal exploration permit and leasing rights on fifteen thousand acres of Cheyenne land. The agreement was the same as for all other companies: 17½ cents a ton for coal shipped off the reservation, 15 cents for coal used on the reservation.

Now, he said, Consol was ready immediately to make the Cheyenne tribe a new offer. The company would increase the royalty on all coal mined to 25 cents a ton, regardless of whether it was used on or off the reservation. The company would pay a bonus of $35 an acre for all land mined. Finally, Consol would make a donation of $1.5 million toward the building of a health center that the Northern Cheyenne so badly needed.

But there would be conditions to this offer. For such a high royalty and large bonus, the tribe would have to agree to let Consolidation Coal Company lease seventy thousand acres of reservation land and mine at least one billion tons of coal. The company would also have to be allowed to build four plants on the reservation. These plants would turn coal into gas, just as generating plants turn coal into electricity. The process of gasification takes a great deal of water, so the tribe would have to agree to let reservation water be used in the plants.

The Consol representative reminded his listeners that the Cheyenne would make a great deal of money from the company's offer. The total royalty on a billion tons of coal would be $250 million. The gasification plants would bring much more money onto the reservation and would mean lots of jobs. The Cheyenne would certainly become one of the richest Indian tribes in America.

Ted Risingsun was in the audience that day when the amazing Consol offer was explained. He remembers breaking into a sweat at the thought of all that money and what he could do with his share of it. But Ted had heard some things about plant building and gasification that he thought his fellow Cheyenne ought to

Ted Risingsun

know, so when a chance came, he stood up to talk.

"Well," he said, "that sure is a lot of money. I've heard that every member of the tribe might get $150,000. And I've heard a few whispers that maybe someday every Cheyenne might even be a millionaire.

"I've been sitting here thinking about what I'd do with all that money, and it's so much I don't really know. But I think one thing I might do is buy myself the most expensive elkskin scalp shirt anybody ever had. You know how our ancestors used to tie scalps on their scalp shirts. Well, I would tie pieces of coal on mine. I'd buy myself the biggest pink Cadillac I could find. Then I'd drive around the country and dance in all the Indian powwows."

The Cheyenne in the room listened quietly. Knowing Ted Risingsun, they knew he had something else on his mind. "But then," Ted continued, "I got to thinking about where I would go when I finished all that dancing. I doubt if I could come back here. We've already leased or given permits to lease over half of our land. If we lease seventy thousand more acres to Consol, there won't be much left. But maybe that's not the main thing. I've heard that to build those gasification plants and run them and take out the coal for them there will be ten white people working and living on this reservation for every Cheyenne here. If that happens, I don't think there will be a Cheyenne tribe any more.

"Now most of us are poor. I don't have to tell anyone in this room about that. But we have these hills and grass and trees and streams, and if we don't give them away, no one can take them away from us. We've got our tribe's whole history and culture right here. So maybe we're not so poor. But even if we are, I think I would rather be poor in my own country, with my own people, with our own way of life than be rich in a torn-up land where I am outnumbered ten to one by strangers."

It was probably the longest speech Ted Risingsun
had ever made, and he could tell from the looks on
the faces of his neighbors and friends and some who
maybe were not friends that they had heard every
word. He knew that the team from Consol had heard,
too, because one of them said that the company had
to have an answer by the next day or the offer would
be withdrawn. Then they left.

The Cheyenne Tribal Council did not answer
Consol the next day or any time soon, but the company
did not withdraw the offer. It was an offer that sent
shock waves through the Tribal Council and into every
Cheyenne home. For the first time the Indians of this
small and isolated tribe began to understand what leasing their land to a big coal company would lead to.
It was not only the stripping bare of a large part of
their land to rip out the coal, though that was bad
enough. But the companies didn't want the coal unless
they could build generating or gasification plants at
the "mine mouth," as company officials expressed it.
Then would come the miners, plant builders, plant
operators, and their families, and the Cheyenne would
become a minority group on their own reservation.

The Consol offer had done another thing. It had
shown the Cheyenne how poorly they had fared finan-
cially under the guidance of the Bureau of Indian Affairs. Consol did not go through the Bureau with its
new offer but rather took it directly to the Cheyenne
Tribal Council. On the BIA's advice the Council had
accepted a 12 cent an acre bonus from the Peabody
Coal Company, and now Consol was offering them
$35 an acre! More important, Consol offered 25 cents

a ton royalty on the coal instead of 17½ cents or 15 cents that all previous leases had called for.

And now it was clear why the coal companies had insisted on that lower royalty of 15 cents for coal burned on the reservation. Their secret plans called for them to burn as much Cheyenne coal as possible on the reservation. The Tribal Council learned that Peabody had plans to mine five hundred million or more tons of coal from their Cheyenne leases and supply it to gasification plants that would be built on or near the reservation by the Northern Gas Company and the City Service Gas Company.

The Tribal Council could understand that in 1966 the BIA might not have known or even guessed at what the coal and power companies' long-range plans were. What the Indians could not understand was why, in time and as interest in Indian coal increased, the Bureau did not learn what was afoot. The BIA, after all, is a part of the Department of the Interior, and it was the Department of the Interior that took the leading role in the *North Central Power Study*. How could two parts of the same department, both concerned with coal in Montana, have no knowledge of what the other was doing?

In a statement before a congressional committee several years later, Allen Rowland, the Council's president, summed up the Cheyenne feeling about the Bureau in these words: "It soon became apparent that the involved BIA personnel, on whose advice and counsel the tribe relied in entering into these transactions, had been inept, uninformed, and sadly overmatched."

Cheyenne adults

Now it was clear to the Cheyenne leaders that the wheel of history had come full circle. There was a terrible symmetry between what had happened to their forefathers a hundred years ago and what was happening to them now. Then the white man had wanted their land for farms and ranches and for the gold beneath the Dakota Black Hills. The government had sent the army cavalry to drive them off the land.

This time, a century later, it was coal that the white man wanted. This time it was not ranchers and farmers and prospectors who came but well-dressed businessmen and lawyers. This time the government could not send the army, for the Cheyenne had legal title to this small piece of land. But the government, in the form of the Bureau of Indian Affairs, could help the businessmen, and it did.

Once again the elders of the Cheyenne tribe recalled the prophecy of Sweet Medicine: "The white people will try to change you from your way of living to theirs, and they will keep at what they try to do. They will tear up the earth and at last you will do it with them. When you do this, you will become crazy and will forget all that I have taught you. Then you will disappear."

The prophecy hung with heavy menace over the heads of the tribal leaders, for now they could see the scarred and torn-up earth around Colstrip only a few miles away. And they themselves had agreed to let the white man tear up Cheyenne land in the same way. *They will tear up the earth and at last you will do it with them.*

Then the tribal leaders knew that they must act.

Perhaps these descendants of Little Wolf and Dull Knife did not hear ancestral voices crying war. Perhaps they did not smoke the medicine pipe and seek guidance in the dreams it brought as Two Moons might have done before the Battle of the Little Bighorn. But they knew one thing: it was time once more for the Cheyenne to fight.

XX   XX   XX   XX

Showdown at Lame Deer

DURING the final months of 1972, Rowland and the rest of the Tribal Council studied the tribe's problem. The beginning of an answer came when Rowland met a young Osage Indian lawyer named George Crossland. Crossland worked for the Bureau of Indian Affairs in Washington but was about to quit his job there.

Rowland told Crossland the whole story of how over half of the Northern Cheyenne reservation had been parceled out in leases and exploration permits to five different coal companies. It was true, he admitted, that the Tribal Council had agreed to the leases and permits. But they had had no idea of what the coal companies were planning to do and had had even less an idea of what their coal was really worth. Rowland asked Crossland to come to Lame Deer and try to help.

Crossland came. The BIA office in Billings thought

he still worked for the Bureau and let him read the files. He studied the leases and permits and reviewed the Code of Federal Regulations on the leasing of Indian lands. He made an important discovery. No study had been made of how strip mining would affect the land, environment, and culture of the Northern Cheyenne tribe. Yet the Code of Federal Regulations states very clearly that the BIA must make such a study before it approves any leases or permits.

Crossland also learned that coal mining leases and permits on Indian lands must not exceed 2,560 acres unless good reasons are given why they should be larger. No reasons were given by the coal companies or the BIA for the huge sizes of the leases and permits on the Northern Cheyenne reservation.

Crossland told the Tribal Council that the BIA had violated government regulations in agreeing to the leases and permits without the technical study and without an explanation from the companies of why they needed so much land. Crossland advised the Council to petition the Secretary of Interior to cancel the agreements. The grounds for cancellation would be that the BIA had not carried out its duties as trustee of Indian lands.

But before a petition could be made, the Tribal Council had to be sure that they could speak with one voice, for each member of the Council is elected by and represents a certain number of tribal members. There were Cheyenne who argued that the agreements with the companies should stand. They said that mining the coal was the only way the tribe could escape from its poverty.

Coal held the promise of decent houses, good
health care, and first class education for the children.
Some Cheyenne would have leased the land they per-
sonally owned except for a law that said all minerals
on the reservation belonged to the tribe as a whole,
even if they were on land that was personal property.

Coal had brought Cheyenne into conflict with
Cheyenne. Some said they could take the coal money
and buy land somewhere else and still have money
left over to help the tribe. But most felt that no amount
of money should make them abandon the home of
their ancestors. Here on a hill overlooking Lame Deer
were buried Dull Knife and Little Wolf. On another
hill nearby was the grave of Two Moons. Here were
the bones and the spirits of Ridge Walker, Stands in
Timber, Medicine Bird, Kills Night, Little Chief, and
so many more. You can sell a homeland, but you can't
buy another.

And so the Cheyenne did as they have always
done. They talked and talked until they came together
in their thinking, and when the time came, the tribe
spoke with a single voice. On March 5, 1973, the Tribal
Council voted eleven to zero to ask the Interior Secretary to cancel all Northern Cheyenne coal leases and
exploration permits.

Later that month the petition landed on Secretary
Rogers Morton's desk like a bombshell. The BIA was
stunned. The coal companies could not believe it. The
general feeling in both the BIA and the coal companies
was that the Cheyenne wanted the leases and permits
cancelled so they could be renegotiated for more
money.

Robert Ridge Walker—Fort Keogh, Montana

"They couldn't believe that our land and environment and culture meant more to us than a stack of
dollars," Ted Risingsun said. "They couldn't believe
it even when we turned down the Consol offer. But
we wanted those agreements cancelled. Period. That
petition was sort of a Cheyenne Declaration of Independence."

Secretary Morton struggled with his decision for
over a year. No Indian tribe had ever challenged the
BIA's conduct like this, and none had ever had a head-
on fight with a group of rich corporations. To tackle
both the government and big business at the same
time was an act of courage to compare with the fiercest
battles of Cheyenne warriors in their struggle with
the army a century earlier.

It was also an act that upset many people in the
Bureau of Indian Affairs. In a later statement about
how some Bureau employees acted, Allen Rowland
said, "In formulating his decision, the Secretary was
subjected to intense lobbying on the part of the BIA
area office and central office personnel responsible for
the formulation and approval of the Northern Cheyenne coal leases who considered the tribe's attack to
be a challenge to their personal reputation, professional
standing, and job security."

In June, 1974, Secretary Morton announced his
ruling. He was careful not to criticize the BIA, and
he did not cancel the leases and permits. But he did
say that there were many legal questions and that there
could be no mining until they were answered. He also
said that there could be no mining until both the coal

companies and the tribe agreed that there should be. In perhaps his most important statement, the Secretary acknowledged his responsibility as trustee to preserve the environment and culture of the Northern Cheyenne, and he said that he would not let anyone's desire to develop the natural resources of the reservation damage the environment or tribal culture.

Secretary Morton's decision was a victory for the Northern Cheyenne, but not a complete victory. No mining would take place now. But the coal companies still had their leases and permits, so the tribe did not have full control over its land. And there was always the possibility that the coal companies would take legal action against the Northern Cheyenne. As in so many of the tribe's battles in the past, they had escaped disaster, but there would be more fighting another day.

In 1975 the giant generating plant called Colstrip One flamed into life, and the following year its twin, Colstrip Two, began operating. Their smokestacks, thirty feet in diameter at the base, thrust themselves over five hundred feet into the sky. Smoke boiled out of them twenty-four hours a day, and from just outside Lame Deer the Indians could see the dirty gray plumes against the blue of the distant sky.

An old man of the tribe, an elder who had once held the Sacred Arrows and who sometimes taught the young men at Bear Butte, looked at the twin smokestacks of Colstrip One and Two and spoke about them. "I think," he said, "that if many of those stood on our land, they would make the sun black. I do not think the Cheyenne could live under a black sun."

The old man spoke the language of his birth, and he called the smokestacks the things that make the sky unclean.

The Cheyenne were curious about Colstrip One and Two, and many went to see the great generating plants. They were awed by the bigness of them, like mountains made by men. Inside, they saw how two hundred tons of coal an hour is moved on a conveyor into each plant and how the coal is turned into electricity by crushing it to a fine powder and blowing it into a gigantic boiler where it burns and changes water into steam. They saw the huge turbine and its steam-driven shaft which is connected to the 350,000 kilowatt generator where the electricity finally is created. And if they did not understand all they saw, they still knew it was a marvelous thing.

But on their way to Colstrip the Cheyenne could see the Big Sky Mine of Peabody Coal and the Rosebud Mine of Western Energy, a company owned by Montana Power. Sometimes they visited the mines and watched the mammoth machines called draglines tear away the earth covering the coal seam. They could hardly believe the size of the draglines. They were told that the biggest dragline stood almost three hundred feet high and that it could pick up enough dirt in one scoopful to fill four railroad boxcars; it could hold twenty automobiles in its giant scoop.

The dirt the dragline dug out, called overburden, was dumped in a long mound. The miners' name for that was the "spoilbank." In the vast pits dug by the dragline, power shovels, their scoops opening and closing like the jaws of prehistoric monsters, dropped huge mouthfuls of coal into waiting trucks.

The Cheyenne looked at the hundreds of acres of scarred and ugly land that had been mined and wondered if it would ever again be good for anything. They were told that, after the coal was mined, the land could be put back the way it was in a process called reclamation. They were shown some reclaimed land and it looked good, but still they wondered. They asked if it would make a difference that the coal was no longer there, since coal helps to hold water in the ground. The reclamation engineer said he did not know and that no one could know for a number of years. It might make a difference.

Colstrip One and Two were hardly in operation when the Cheyenne Tribal Council received some information that troubled them very much. Montana Power and three West Coast power companies were going to build two more generating plants at Colstrip. These plants would be known as Colstrip Three and Four. Each one of these new plants would be as big as Colstrip One and Two combined! Each one would produce 700,000 kilowatts of electricity. Their smokestacks would tower two hundred feet above those of Colstrip One and Two. The stripping of coal in the area around the Northern Cheyenne reservation would rise to twenty million tons each year.

(Overleaf) Colstrip—coal being brought for processing
(Inset) Cheyenne tipple operator at Big Sky Mine

The northern boundary of the Cheyenne reservation is only twelve miles from Colstrip. Looking at Colstrip One and Two, the Indians tried to imagine what the sky would look like with three times that much smoke pouring into it. They tried to imagine what the air over their reservation would be like when the wind blew from the north. And they knew this was not the end. There would be Colstrip Five and Six or other plants like them until one day generating and gasification plants would surround the Cheyenne reservation like an army laying siege.

Once more the leaders of the tribe knew that it was time to act. They had protected their land from the coal companies, at least for the time being, but how could they protect the air above them? The possibility of an answer came as they talked over the problem with ranchers and environmental groups in eastern Montana that were also deeply worried about unrestricted strip mining and coal burning in generating and gasification plants.

Out of their discussions came the idea that the Cheyenne might apply to the Environmental Protection Agency in Washington for a "Class One" clean air designation for their reservation. Under the new federal Clean Air Act industries were legally responsible for keeping air pollution caused by their factories and plants within certain limits. The act also specifies that the air in certain places such as national parks and national forests is to be kept as pure as possible, and these places are given Class One clean air classifications.

Most people assumed that the Class One category

was for special public places like Yellowstone National Park and the Grand Canyon. But with the help of a good Seattle law firm that had also helped them with their petition to the Secretary of Interior, the Tribal Council asked the Environmental Protection Agency to give the Northern Cheyenne reservation a Class One clean air classification.

They argued that pure air was a part of the Cheyenne heritage, as much a part of the life they had chosen to live as the clear sky above them and the pine-clad hills around them. By living here, they were giving up many benefits and pleasures of city life; clean air was one benefit they should not have to give up.

The Council had expected long bureaucratic delays in a response to their request. To their surprise, but much to their happiness, the Environmental Protection Agency quickly gave the Northern Cheyenne reservation a Class One clean air designation.

That was step one, but by itself it meant very little. The next step was to use their Class One designation to keep Montana Power from building Colstrip Three and Four. The very idea of it was frightening, but they asked the Environmental Protection Agency to deny building rights to Montana Power for Colstrip Three and Four on the grounds that the pollution would violate their reservation's Class One clean air classification.

Ted Risingsun knows a great deal about the Cheyenne religion, but he is also a practicing Christian and sometimes Biblical references spice his conversation. "I think maybe I know how David felt with his slingshot when he looked up at Goliath," he said, recalling

those days of conflict with Montana Power. "Imagine
a little Indian tribe like ours telling four of the biggest
power companies in the West that we didn't want any
more of their generating plants around our reservation.
Most people thought Goliath would step on us and
that would be the end of it."

The situation did look hopeless when, in 1978,
the Environmental Protection Agency announced that
it intended to approve the Montana Power group's
request to build Colstrip Three and Four. But the Cheyenne did not give up. With the help of their friends
they brought in experts who made a study of what
the air would be like if Colstrip Three and Four were
built and had the same pollution controls as Colstrip
One and Two.

When the study was finished, the Cheyenne took
it to the Environmental Protection Agency. The study
showed that the level of pollution would definitely
violate their reservation's Class One pure air rating.
In a decision that delighted the Cheyenne and shocked
the power companies, the Environmental Protection
Agency announced that it would not issue building
permits for Colstrip Three and Four.

Montana Power was furious. In a statement to
the press, the company's executive vice president said,
"We've already spent $130 million getting ready to
build them and they are so badly needed that we do
not intend to stop now."

The fight was bitter. Some people called the
Northern Cheyenne selfish, and others said the eastern
part of Montana might have to be considered a "national sacrifice area" for the rest of the country that

needed energy so much. But most people admired the Cheyenne for their determination to protect their tribal heritage, and many economists criticized the coal and power companies for hasty and unplanned actions. They said it was a good idea to slow down and plan the development of coal resources more carefully.

The Cheyenne Tribal Council knew very well that the fight was far from over. The power companies immediately appealed the Environmental Protection Agency's decision. The Agency reviewed the case once more and said that permits to build and operate Colstrip Three and Four could be granted if the power companies would install more effective pollution control equipment. The technology for better control was available, but it would be expensive.

The power companies had another idea. They went to court with a lawsuit challenging the Northern Cheyenne's right to a Class One clean air classification for their reservation. If the companies could get the Cheyenne classification changed to a lower rating, they would not have to install the more expensive pollution control equipment. So the court fight began.

Now, the Tribal Council decided, it was time to get back to another fight, the cancellation of all coal leases and permits on the Cheyenne reservation. Rowland and other Council members met with a number of politicians who were known for their fair and thoughtful handling of Indian problems. Out of these meetings came a new and dramatic idea: why not try to get a bill passed in Congress cancelling the coal leases and permits?

From his discussion with tribal leaders, Senator

John Melcher of Montana was convinced that injustice
had been done to the Northern Cheyenne tribe, and
he agreed to sponsor the bill. In March, 1980, the Sen-
ate Select Committee on Indian Affairs met in Billings,
Montana, to consider the bill. The meeting was chaired
by Senator Melcher. The Cheyenne tribe was represented by Allen Rowland. All of the companies with
leases and exploration permits on the Cheyenne reservation had representatives at the meeting, and an official from the Bureau of Indian Affairs was there.

Senator Melcher opened the meeting, reviewed
the history of the leases and permits, and spoke of
the Tribal Council's petition to the Secretary of Interior
for cancellation. Then Senator Melcher said, "This bill
I have introduced is to do what the Secretary could
have done, I believe, and probably should have done,
six years ago. That is to cancel the coal leases and
permits on the basis that they were entered into in a
manner that violated the federal government's trust
responsibility to the tribe."

Those were strong words, but they seemed lost
on the official from the BIA, who asked to speak next.
He said that the Interior Department was strongly op-
posed to the idea of an act of Congress to cancel the
leases and permits on the Northern Cheyenne reservation. Interior felt that the Cheyenne and the coal companies should settle their dispute by negotiation. Then
the BIA official said, "We believe this measure is both
unjustified and unnecessary and would set a bad prece-
dent for future similar situations that may arise."

In short, the Interior Department and the BIA
were very nervous about Congress overriding the De-

partment's authority, and they were unhappy at the bill's clear statement that the BIA had not carried out its trust responsibility properly.

When Allen Rowland's turn to speak came, he introduced a memorandum listing thirty-six violations of the Code of Federal Regulations by the coal companies. Then he made a powerful statement condemning the Bureau of Indian Affairs and the Interior Department. He concluded by saying: "We think that each company would recognize that any rights to develop coal on the Northern Cheyenne reservation are, in fact, meaningless unless enthusiastically supported by the Northern Cheyenne people as a whole."

Rowland continued: "It is now absolutely clear that no such support exists for these transactions. During the initial stages of our struggle against these transactions, and, indeed, for several years thereafter, many governmental and industry people believed that the real purpose of the tribe's effort was to extract larger monetary payments from the coal companies through a forced renegotiation. However, for some time now, that cynical view has been discredited. It is now recognized that the tribe has acted pursuant to its own sense of duty and honor, the duty to protect and preserve the Northern Cheyenne reservation as a homeland for the Northern Cheyenne people."

It should be said that all of the coal companies at the meeting seemed to understand what Allen Rowland was saying, and all agreed that an act of Congress cancelling the leases and permits was probably the best action to take. They also agreed that a fair solution might be to let the companies lease a limited amount of government-owned coal land, at a fair market value, in return for the Northern Cheyenne land they would lose.

Jim Reger, one of the company representatives, seemed to speak for all of them when he said: "We know the Northern Cheyenne don't want us to mine coal down there. We found that out years ago, and we don't want a big fight or any more litigation than there has been. We are willing to walk away. All we care about is some equitable type arrangement, some solution to this. The Indians need that so they can get on down the road with their plans."

The bill to cancel the coal leases and permits was passed by Congress and signed into law by President Jimmy Carter on October 9, 1980. At last their reservation was again under the control of the Northern Cheyenne tribe. They were poor as they had always been. They had turned their backs on great riches. But the land was still beautiful, still unscarred by dragline and power shovel. The air was pure, and the sun had not turned black.

"We Must Help Ourselves"

A FTER Paul and I had been on the Northern Cheyenne reservation for a week, we had a long talk with Joe Little Coyote. Joe is one of the busiest people on the reservation, but the things we were talking about go to the very heart of why he came back to the reservation after his years at Harvard. He took his time and spoke his mind fully.

"Some members of the Northern Cheyenne tribe are afraid that Sweet Medicine's prophecy has already literally come to pass," he said. "The Cheyenne were once a proud and self-sufficient people, like an independent nation. Now we are 99 percent dependent on the federal government for everything we have, and it's been that way for a hundred years.

"There's an Indian Education Act, an Indian Finance Act, an Indian Health Care Act, an Indian Community College Act, a BIA Indian Youth Conservation Corps Program, an Indian Housing Improvement Pro-

Joe Little Coyote

gram, an Indian Action Program—and that's just a few of them. Every act and program is tied up with a hundred regulations. Indians in this country are more heavily regulated than the airlines, and there's an army of BIA and other government people to do the regulating."

"But surely these programs are for the purpose of helping Indians," I said.

"That's not the point," Joe Little Coyote answered, "or I guess maybe it is the point. If you let somebody help you all the time, you lose control. Maybe the reason he is helping you is so he can keep control of you, or maybe it isn't. The result is the same. You become less and less of what you could potentially be because he is in control. You keep doing things his way and eventually you forget who you really are. Finally, you become just like him.

"Every American Indian tribe is caught in the dependency trap, but we are talking about the Northern Cheyenne now. Sweet Medicine's prophecy was really about loss of identity. He was saying to his people that if they let the white man control them, they would start to act like the white man, and then they wouldn't be a Cheyenne people. They would forget who they were, and finally they would disappear as a people."

"You said some Cheyenne think that has already happened," I reminded Joe. "Do you think it has happened?"

He was silent for a moment. "No, I don't," he said. "But it can happen and it will happen unless we break out of Fort Dependency like Dull Knife and his people broke out of Fort Robinson a hundred years ago."

"And how will you do that?" I asked.

Joe Little Coyote said, "The Tribal Council and all the other Cheyenne leaders know that the only hope of preserving Cheyenne identity is through developing self-reliance. We must help ourselves. That doesn't mean we will close our eyes and ears to the outside world. We know we're a part of America and we know our economy is tied up with the national economy. But from now on we intend to see that Cheyenne affairs and the Cheyenne economy will be directed and controlled by members of the Cheyenne tribe. We must determine our own destiny."

"Was getting your land back from the coal companies a first step in that direction?" I asked.

Joe smiled. "That was the big step," he said. "Other steps will be just as hard, but now we know we can take them if we want to badly enough."

Paul gets restless if he goes very long without taking a picture. I saw him looking around Joe Little Coyote's office. It was in an expandable trailer, and the furnishings consisted of desks for himself, an assistant, and a secretary. A few hard-backed chairs (borrowed, Joe said) were scattered around, and the walls were covered with maps of the reservation.

"Do you mind if I take some pictures?" Paul asked.

"I don't see much to take," Joe said, "but go ahead. Just don't shoot the maps. That's against our agreement with ARCO."

Paul stood up and started shooting Joe, the secretary, the assistant, and anyone else who opened the office door.

I knew that Joe was head of the Northern Cheyenne Oil and Gas Office. "I've heard about the tribe's agreement with the ARCO Oil and Gas Company," I said. "Is that another big step for the tribe?"

"It is," Joe replied. "We've learned a lot in the last few years, and we know now that economic self-sufficiency for the tribe lies in the wise development and investment of our resources."

(Above and overleaf) Cheyenne school children

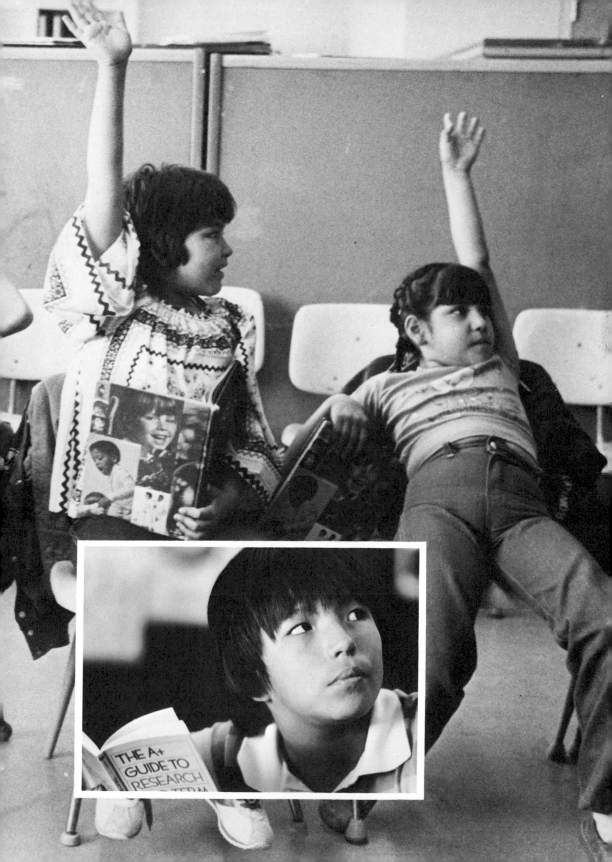

"But you took your coal back from the companies that wanted to develop it," I said.

"The way it was going to be developed wouldn't have been wise development," Joe said. "We would have ruined our land, our air, and our culture for a lot of quick dollars. We may develop our coal someday, but if we do, it will be in a way and at a pace that suits us." He paused and added, "I see Mother Earth with her resources as a nourisher, just as a mother nourishes her child. We love our land and want to take care of it. And if we do, we know that the land will take care of us."

"Can you tell me about the ARCO agreement?" I asked.

"No one knows whether oil and gas are on our land in commercial quantities," Joe said, "but there are some indications that they might be. If they are and if oil and gas wells are sunk, they won't tear up the land like strip mining would and they won't bring in crowds of outsiders.

"The tribe invited oil companies to make exploration offers, and thirty companies bid. We took the two best offers, but they were standard models of what oil companies have always had on Indian lands. You know, leases lasting forever, royalties as little as they can make them, no adjustment clauses, and everything else slanted in the company's favor.

"We told those two companies that the tribe had a list of its own, a list of things we wanted addressed by the companies before we would seriously consider their proposals. We wanted protection of the environment and protection of historical and cultural areas.

We wanted employment assurances for Cheyenne tribal members and on-the-job training for them. Most important, we did not want a lease and royalty arrangement. We wanted a contract with the company that would give us some control over what took place in development, and we wanted a percentage of all oil and gas production."

"It sounds like you had some good bargainers and negotiators working for you," I commented.

Joe Little Coyote laughed. "We did the bargaining this time," he said. "We left the BIA out of it. They didn't like that a bit, but we were signing a service agreement, not a land lease that would have created property rights for ARCO. Because of their trust responsibility, we still had to get BIA approval. We got it, but it wasn't easy."

"You did the bargaining with ARCO?" I asked.

"Allen Rowland did most of it," Joe said, "and he's a hard bargainer, I'll tell you that. I was there, too, and maybe the course I took at Harvard called 'The Art of Negotiations' helped a little."

"And how did it come out?" I asked.

"We got what we wanted," Joe said. "ARCO finally made the best offer. We got a 25 percent production-sharing arrangement of gross production, and they pay all costs out of their share. We got employment and training for tribal members, environmental and cultural protection, and other things. And ARCO offered an upfront bonus of $6 million just for the privilege of doing business with the tribe. We get that whether ARCO finds any oil or gas or not. We also get annual rental payments of $1⅓ million upfront.

We can use that money, and we can learn a lot from this partnership, even if we don't hit any big oil pools or gas fields."

As we left Joe's office, Paul said, "In his book, *The Rape of the Great Plains,* Professor Toole calls the Northern Cheyenne the most important tribe in America today because of the example they have set for other Indian tribes by standing up to the government and big business to fight for what they believe in. What do you think of that?"

Joe Little Coyote frowned. "I'm not sure what the professor means by important," he said, "but I do know there are at least twenty-five other Indian tribes in America that face the same pressures we faced because they have coal, oil, gas, or uranium on their land. If they can learn something from what has happened to us and what we've done about it, I guess that's important."

At the trailer door, I turned back. "I know I'll have some more questions," I said. "I wonder if I could see you again tomorrow."

"Not tomorrow," Joe Little Coyote said. "Tomorrow a planeload of Indians from a bunch of tribes is landing at the St. Labre Mission airstrip. I have to meet them and bring them back here." Joe grinned. "They want to talk about the Cheyenne agreement with ARCO."

On April 21, 1980, the Northern Cheyenne took one more step toward self-reliance and protection of their land. On that date they signed an agreement with

Montana Power and the three other companies that wanted to build the Colstrip Three and Four generating plants. In 1979 the companies agreed to install the highest level of pollution control equipment at Colstrip Three and Four, and on that basis the Environmental Protection Agency issued building permits for the new plants. The Northern Cheyenne brought a lawsuit against the Agency for issuing the permit.

Under the agreement signed by the tribe and the power companies in 1980, the Northern Cheyenne dropped their lawsuit against the Environmental Protection Agency. On their part, the power companies agreed to maintain the highest level of air pollution control for as long as Colstrip Three and Four were in operation, even if the Northern Cheyenne Class One clean air classification should be lowered in the future to Class Two.

"We got the best deal we could," said a member of the Tribal Council. "Winning that lawsuit against the EPA was just about impossible."

Wally McRae, a rancher who had watched the long fight of the Cheyenne against the power companies, said to Paul, "We should thank the Indians. Because of them Colstrip Three and Four will be three times cleaner than Colstrip One and Two. You could run them in downtown Seattle."

There was much more to the settlement. The companies agreed to install three high-technology air quality monitoring stations on the Cheyenne reservation and to provide funds to train tribal members to operate them. The agreement also called for a program to hire

Dennis Limberhand

Cheyenne to work in the Colstrip generating plants
and the mines and to provide on-the-job training so
that they could work themselves into technical and
higher-level administrative positions. The Western Energy Company official in charge of the program is Dennis Limberhand, himself a Northern Cheyenne. Already more than a hundred Northern Cheyenne have
worked at the Colstrip plants and mines.

"We're taking money back to the reservation,"
one of the workers said, "but it's more important than
that. Someday, when we're ready to mine our own
coal, we'll know an awful lot about how to do it."

Paul stayed on the reservation after I left, taking
more pictures. One of the things he wanted to see
was an air monitoring station. Sylvester Knows Gun
took him. They drove to a place on the northern
boundary, the highest point on the reservation. It was
cool in that high place, Paul said, and the wind rustled
the needles of the ponderosa pines.

Sylvester Knows Gun pointed to a silver trailer
standing on the crest of the rise. "That's the monitoring
station," he said. "It's not big but it's powerful. It has
everything to let us watch them like a hawk, and that's
what we will do. There's no point in living in a beautiful place like this unless the air is clean."

Mr. Knows Gun is head of the Tribal Planning
Office, a new organization put together by the Tribal
Council to help in the drive for development and self-
sufficiency. Within the Planning Office are the Environmental Affairs Department, Research Department,
and Economic Development Projects Department.

But that day on the high hill overlooking ancient

Cheyenne land, Sylvester Knows Gun seemed to be thinking not about development plans but about the tribal legacy of cleanliness.

"Cleanliness is woven into all the rest of our culture," he said to Paul. "Clean body; we still purify ourselves in sweat lodges, just as our ancestors did. Water unpolluted. Minds uncluttered; some Cheyenne still make the trip to Bear Butte in remembrance of the teachings of Maheo and to purify their minds and spirits. The air must be pure to breathe and clear to see the brightness of the sun and stars."

Paul had seen a great deal of sky and sun in the weeks he had been in that high Montana country. But, he told me later, as he stood there with Sylvester Knows Gun, with smoke from the great stacks of Colstrip One and Two hanging in the far distance, the sky above the Northern Cheyenne reservation seemed an even more brilliant blue than usual and the sun just a little brighter.

Cheyenne construction workers at Colstrip 4

To Be Cheyenne

O N this Friday night the brightly lighted gymnasium in Lame Deer is alive with noise and activity. Small children laugh and scream as they chase each other around the outer edges of the basketball court playing tag or simply scuffling. Men and women stand talking in small groups or sit in the bleachers lining both sides of the court. In one corner a concession stand does a brisk business in hamburgers, hot dogs, cold drinks, and coffee. At a nearby table, women crowd around to place small bets on a card game.

This might be a social gathering in any gymnasium in America except for one thing. In the middle of the gym floor two small bleachers of five tiers each face each other. A blaring voice on the loudspeaker calls out names and nags people to take their places. Finally, the two small bleachers are filled with men and women of all ages, including a few teenagers, and the first round of a hand game is about to begin. Eight teams are entered in this contest, six from the Northern Cheyenne reservation and two from the nearby Crow reservation. In the complicated double elimination system, they will play late into the night, most of Saturday, and perhaps part of Sunday before the winning team is decided.

With the possible exception of horse racing, the hand game is the most popular Cheyenne sport. It is a game in which a member of one team tries to guess the hand in which a member of the opposing team is hiding a small piece of bone. With each correct guess a team wins a stick from a pile of fourteen game sticks. The sticks are passed back and forth until one team wins them all. A game might end in a few minutes, but it might last for two hours or more.

To an outsider, the hand game might seem simple and not very exciting. But it is an ancient Indian game full of skill and, some believe, magic. Some players develop great skill in hiding the bone, but the most prized ability in a player is that of guessing the hand which holds the bone. Any man, woman, or child who has proved that he or she has that ability is welcome on a team.

Every team has a medicine man who decides who will hide the bone and who will guess. The medicine man also tries to place a hex on the other team, to take away their magic. Probably most people today do not really believe there is magic in the game but trying to hex the other team is part of the fun, as is the chanting and pounding of drums that accompanies the efforts of both teams. The team that wins the con-

Cheyenne hand game

Medicine man James Black Wolf conducts ceremony using medicine pipe.

test receives a money prize, and as the games progress, the excitement becomes quite feverish.

The hand game is an example of how the Cheyenne keep an old custom alive in their life in the late twentieth century. It is the same game that their ancestors played a hundred or even two hundred years ago by campfires during buffalo hunt feasts. Today they play the hand game in a gymnasium and eat hamburgers and hot dogs. A hundred years ago the Crows were their deadly enemies whom they met in bloody battles. Today their rivalry with the Crows is in the hand game, horse racing, and basketball, and it is more friendly than not.

Many other social customs of the past remain a part of Northern Cheyenne life. Powwows are held several times a year. In the past most Cheyenne dances were for sacred purposes: to ask Maheo's blessing in battle, to bring the buffalo, to renew the power of the Sacred Arrows. But dancing was also done for fun in olden times when men of the warrior societies— Fox Soldiers, Dog Soldiers, Red Shields, Bowstrings— would come together to see who could dance best and to impress young women of the tribe.

Today dancing at powwows is mostly for enjoyment, but the sacred element is always present in prayers to ask the protection of the All Father. The powwow remains an occasion that is uniquely Indian and that always brings the Northern Cheyenne tribe together. Tribal members who no longer live on the reservation come back for the good-time powwows of summer, and their Oklahoma cousins, the Southern Cheyenne, often come. People from other tribes such as the Sioux also come to the Northern Cheyenne powwows.

Giveaways are still a part of Northern Cheyenne social life and usually take place during powwows. Horses are seldom given away any more, but a family having a giveaway will present blankets and clothes to friends, to persons who have helped them, and to people they admire.

Lost in thought—a young powwow dancer

In some cases the Northern Cheyenne have integrated their celebrations into those of the white world, and the most important times for powwows and giveaways now are Christmas and the Fourth of July. Speaking of the Fourth of July celebration, one young Cheyenne who had fought in Vietnam said, "The United States is our country, too, and maybe we know more than most other Americans what the land means to us."

Schoolboys practice arrow throwing in Lame Deer.

The Cheyenne world today is a mixture of the Indian world and the white world. Except for a few very old people, everyone speaks English, but most Cheyenne still speak the Cheyenne language and often prefer it to English when there is no outsider present. Yet more and more young Cheyenne have only a partial knowledge of the tribal language, and a few cannot speak it at all.

Times have changed since those days when Chey-

enne children were punished for playing Indian games
and speaking their language in school. Today they
practice the hand game and throw the Cheyenne arrow
as a part of their recreation program. Now Cheyenne
is taught as a subject in the schools at Lame Deer
and Busby, and children are made to feel that it is
good to speak their own language.

Ralph Red Fox is a man who has thought long
and hard about what it means to be Cheyenne and
what will be necessary to preserve the Cheyenne people as a tribe. "Language is so important," he said to
Paul and me. "There are things about our beliefs and
our history that can be talked about best in Cheyenne.
To truly be Cheyenne we must know the language
of Sweet Medicine, Erect Horns, and Morning Star.
We do not have to speak it all the time, but we must
be able to speak it any time we want to.

"But learning and speaking Cheyenne is hard
when every day you hear nothing but English on television, on radio, in movies, and in school. My oldest
children speak Cheyenne. My youngest understand it
but do not speak it. I think that is my fault."

Ralph's main concern is the education of Cheyenne children. "There is almost nothing in textbooks
to help a Cheyenne child understand better who he
is and who his people were and are. And there are
very few Cheyenne teachers in the schools. We must
have more. The white philosophy taught in the schools
is that man should go out and conquer the earth. The
Cheyenne child learns at home that man is a caretaker
of the earth. It is very confusing for him."

Tom Gardner was a member of the Tribal Council

Ralph Red Fox

Tom Gardner, Jr., in Birney

when he was twenty-one years old, the youngest person ever elected to the Council. Now, twenty-five years later, he is pastor of the Mennonite Church at the little Cheyenne settlement of Birney on the Tongue River. The pressures on young Cheyenne and the confusions they face is one of his major concerns, and he makes a point similar to the one made by Ralph Red Fox.

"White children," he says, "are brought up to put their money in piggy banks and to compete against all others in society to make their mark. Cheyenne children are taught to share, and they are taught that making a mark is not worth hurting another Cheyenne."

An old Cheyenne, one who went with other Cheyenne children to a BIA school off the reservation sixty years ago, tells a story that illustrates Tom Gardner's point very well. "If a teacher asked a pupil a question and he didn't know the answer, she would scold him or maybe hit him with a ruler, and then she would ask someone else. But even if we knew the answer, we wouldn't say anything because we didn't want to hurt the feelings of the boy who didn't know the answer. So we kept quiet and took a scolding or got hit with the ruler."

It is hard to get young Cheyenne to talk about themselves. You have the feeling that they don't think of themselves as different or special and that they don't want other people to think of them that way. They have dances, play basketball, sing in glee clubs, ride motorbikes, drive cars like young people everywhere in the country. Yet they know that far too many of

Pam Little Wolf

their friends drop out of school, and they know that alcohol and drug use are serious problems. Living in two cultures at the same time is not easy.

And the young Cheyenne know that they are, after all, special because they are Cheyenne. They have a heritage that is theirs alone. They have a history in which names like Sweet Medicine and Dull Knife are more directly important to what they are and who they are than the names of George Washington and Abraham Lincoln.

Pamela Little Wolf is a senior at the Busby high school. She intends to go to college somewhere in Montana when she graduates. "I am proud to be a Cheyenne," she says. "I intend to come back here after college. I want to live and work here on the reservation."

Miller Crazy Mule is also a student at Busby. It has not been easy for him. "I'm gonna try to make it," he says. Nothing more.

Tom Gardner, Jr., goes to the high school in Colstrip, a school that has mostly white students. He gets along all right, plays baseball, plays the guitar, and listens to rock music. But he knows that the world of his white classmates is not really his world. He wonders why the textbooks he studies say little or nothing about Indians. He is happiest when he is hunting in the hills around Birney.

Anthony Littlewhirlwind is a freshman at Dull Knife Memorial College in Lame Deer. He is a great-great-grandson of Little Wolf. His family lives in California now, and when he was eighteen he joined the navy and travelled to a number of countries. "I was drawn back here to Lame Deer to find out who I am," he says. "A search for ancient boundaries. I doubt if I will stay. The pull of the outside world is too strong. This is a temporary stop, a way station. At least I feel that way now."

Ted Risingsun's grandmother was Broken Foot Woman, one of four daughters of a Pawnee wife of Dull Knife. She was thirteen when she started the long trek back to Montana from Oklahoma. Later she lived in a tiny log cabin in Busby until she died in 1942. When Ted was a child, his grandmother told him and his friends many stories which he vividly remembers.

Miller Crazy Mule

Anthony Littlewhirlwind (left) in biology lab at Dull Knife Memorial College

She told of bloody footprints in the snow on the flight north. The stronger men would break trail in the frozen snow, which would turn red as the ice shards pierced their bare feet. Broken Foot Woman would cry when she recalled the bloody snow. Her mother was killed by a stampeding horse which ran over her as she slept on the snowy ground. Traveling Woman, one of Broken Foot Woman's sisters, was shot in the back by a soldier during the escape from Fort Robinson.

When Ted Risingsun told us these stories, we knew that he was making a special point. He was reminding us that the most dramatic period in Northern Cheyenne history is very close to the tribe today. It is as if we had a grandmother who told us how she had wrapped bandages for the soldiers at Valley Forge or a grandfather who could describe the sound of Lincoln's voice as he spoke at Gettysburg.

The leaders of the Northern Cheyenne today believe that their efforts to bring back the self-reliance and the self-sufficiency of the past to their tribe will be successful. They also believe that the tribe's tragic and heroic past is alive in the soul of every Cheyenne and creates an innate will to survive. They believe that this sense of their past and a newfound economic independence will come together to ensure a strong Northern Cheyenne tribe for the rest of this century and into the next.

And the prophecy of Sweet Medicine that the tribe would disappear?

"I don't think it was meant to be a pronouncement of certain doom," Joe Little Coyote said during our talk in his office. "I believe it was to warn us and guide us. Every generation of Northern Cheyenne must have strength to fight for survival or we will disappear. Sweet Medicine told us we must not forget who we are. Well, we do not intend to forget."

Further Reading About the Northern Cheyenne and Western Coal Development

For the reader who wants to learn more about the Northern Cheyenne and about the problems and possibilities of developing the American West's great coal reserves, we have several suggestions. *The Fighting Cheyennes* by George Bird Grinnell is an interesting history of the Cheyenne tribe with much information about their customs and everyday ways of life in the nineteenth century. *Cheyenne Autumn* by Mari Sandoz tells with deep feeling the story of the Northern Cheyenne's removal to Oklahoma and their heroic return to their Montana homeland. *The Rape of the Great Plains* by Kenneth Ross Toole and *Last Stand on the Rosebud* by Michael Parfit are recent books that explore fully what the development of Western coal will mean in human and national economic terms.

Index